Pendle's Curse

The RIP Squad Chronicles

Blake Patrick

CONTENTS

Dedication

To my beloved grandchildren,

This book is dedicated to you - the bright sparks of hope and joy in my life. May these pages fill your hearts with wonder, fuel your imaginations, and remind you always of the power of curiosity and courage.

In every mystery solved by the RIP Squad, see the reflection of your own potential for adventure and discovery. Let their journey inspire you to explore, question, and embrace the unknown with open arms and brave hearts.

Remember, the world is full of stories waiting to be uncovered, and each of you carries the light to illuminate the shadows. May you always find the strength to face your fears, the wisdom to seek the truth, and the warmth of love and family to guide you through life's adventures.

With all my love,

Pops

Preface

In the heart of an ordinary town lies an extraordinary story, one that weaves the threads of history, mystery, and the unexplained into a tapestry as rich as it is real. "Pendle's Curse – The RIP Squad Chronicles" invites you on a captivating adventure through the streets of Hillview Gardens, a place where the past is not just remembered, but deeply felt.

This story is about more than just the supernatural. It is a tale of resilience, unity, and the indomitable human spirit. At its centre is the RIP Squad (Retired Investigators of the Paranormal), a group of individuals whose curiosity and courage lead them to confront the shadows lurking in their midst. They are not professional ghost hunters or seasoned paranormal experts. Instead, they are neighbours, friends, and community members who find themselves entwined in a series of events that challenge their understanding of the world and their place within it.

The genesis of this journey begins with an unsettling occurrence at Hillview Gardens, a seemingly idyllic community that harbours a deep, hidden connection to the Pendle Witch Trials of the 17th century. As the RIP Squad delves deeper into the mystery, they uncover secrets long buried and truths long forgotten. What starts as a quest to understand strange happenings soon becomes a mission to bring peace to restless spirits and resolution to a community grappling with the unknown.

In these pages, you will encounter moments of fear, suspense, and revelation. You will meet characters who are as complex as they are courageous, each playing a part in unravelling the mysteries of Hillview Gardens. From the determined leadership of Jack to the insightful wisdom of Sienna, the medium, each member of the RIP Squad brings their unique strengths to bear against the challenges they face.

But beyond the thrills and chills of a ghostly tale lies a deeper narrative. This book is also a reflection on history's impact on the present, the power of collective memory, and the importance of facing our fears. It is a reminder that sometimes, in order to move forward, we must first confront the past.

As you turn these pages, allow yourself to be transported to Hillview Gardens, to walk in the shoes of the RIP Squad, and to experience the extraordinary journey that lies within the ordinary. Welcome to "Pendle's Curse – The RIP Squad Chronicles."

1

THE NEW ESTATE

The early morning sun cast a gentle glow over Pendle Hill, illuminating the new housing estate at its base. It was a picturesque scene, one of tranquility and promise. The estate, named "Hillview Gardens," boasted modern architecture that blended seamlessly with the lush greenery surrounding it. Families, young couples, and retirees alike were starting to move in, each drawn by the allure of a fresh start in a serene setting.

At the heart of Hillview Gardens stood a grand old oak tree, its branches stretching wide as if to embrace the newcomers. Underneath its protective canopy, children played, their laughter mingling with the chirping of birds and the rustling of leaves. Parents unpacked boxes and arranged furniture, occasionally stopping to exchange pleasantries with their new neighbours. There was an air of communal harmony, a shared sense of embarking on a new chapter together.

But not everything was as it seemed.

As the day wore on, subtle oddities began to emerge. Shadows seemed to linger a little longer than natural, and the wind carried whispers that sounded almost like hushed conversations. The old oak tree, while majestic by day, took on an eerie presence as dusk approached, its gnarled limbs casting unsettling shapes onto the ground.

The first to notice these peculiarities was Emma, a young mother who had moved in with her husband and two children. While unpacking in her new kitchen, she felt a sudden chill, despite the warm summer air. She shrugged it off as a draft, but the feeling of being watched lingered.

Next door, retired police officer Jack, part of the future RIP Squad (Retired Investigators of the Paranormal), observed a strange mist hovering over the ground. It was subtle, almost imperceptible, but it seemed to move against the wind rather than with it. Jack, a man of logic and reason, dismissed it as a trick of the light. Yet, something in the back of his mind cautioned him to remain alert.

As night fell, the sense of unease grew. The streetlights flickered intermittently, casting the estate into temporary darkness. In those brief moments, the residents felt an inexplicable sense of dread, as if the night itself was alive with unseen watchers.

In one of the houses, a child woke up screaming from a nightmare, speaking of a "lady in the shadows" who whispered secrets in a language he couldn't understand. His parents, bleary-eyed and concerned, soothed him back to sleep, attributing the dream to the stress of moving.

At the stroke of midnight, a collective shiver ran down the spine of the estate. Dogs howled in unison, and the wind carried a mournful cry that seemed to come from the hill itself. The residents, each in their own home, pulled their blankets a little tighter, trying to shake off the feeling of cold fingers brushing against their skin.

Hillview Gardens, with its modern façades and well-manicured lawns, was supposed to be a haven, a place of new beginnings. But as the first night drew to a close, a whispering voice seemed to drift through the air, a remnant of a long-forgotten past, hinting that some beginnings are born from endings long buried and best forgotten.

And so, as the first rays of dawn broke the horizon, the residents of Hillview Gardens awoke to their new life, unaware that the true story of their home was yet to unfold, a story woven with threads of mystery, history, and an unshakable chill that promised to reveal itself in the most haunting of ways.

As the morning sun rose higher, dispelling the last shadows of the night, the residents of Hillview Gardens began their day, each trying to shake off the remnants of unease from the night before. The estate buzzed with activity: children excitedly exploring their new surroundings, and adults engaged in the final touches of setting up their homes.

In house number 12, Emma stood by her kitchen window, sipping her coffee. She couldn't help but feel a lingering sense of discomfort from the previous night. Her gaze drifted towards the old oak tree, its leaves glistening with dew. Something about it felt off, though she couldn't pinpoint what. Emma decided to dismiss these thoughts as mere side effects of the stress of moving.

2

THE RIP SQUAD

Across the street, in house number 7, Jack, the retired police officer, sat in his study, surrounded by unpacked boxes. He was a man who believed in facts and evidence, yet the strange occurrences of the previous night had left him unsettled. He made a mental note to keep an eye out for any further oddities. Jack had always been intrigued by the unexplainable, a trait that had led him to form the RIP Squad. The RIP Squad (The Retired Investigators of the Paranormal), led by Jack, was a group of former law enforcement professionals who had developed a keen interest in paranormal investigations after their retirement. Each member brought a unique skill set to the group - from investigative experience to forensic expertise. The group was formed as a hobby but soon grew into a serious endeavour, with regular meetings and discussions on various unexplained phenomena they had read about or encountered.

Upon hearing about the strange occurrences in Hillview Gardens, particularly the message on the wall, the RIP Squad saw an opportunity to apply their skills in a real-world situation. They convened in Jack's garage, which had been converted into a makeshift command centre, filled with monitors, maps, and various pieces of equipment. The walls were lined with bookshelves holding an extensive collection of texts on paranormal investigations, forensics, and criminal psychology.

The team started with a strategic planning session. They mapped out the estate, highlighting the locations of reported activities. They discussed potential approaches, considering both the scientific and the supernatural angles. Their plan was methodical - first to gather data and then to analyse it for patterns and possible explanations.

The RIP Squad was equipped with a range of technology typically used in paranormal investigations. They had EMF (electromagnetic field) meters, infrared cameras, digital voice recorders for capturing EVPs (Electronic Voice Phenomena), and thermal imaging cameras. They also had a collection of more traditional tools like compasses, dowsing rods, and a library of historical records and maps.

Their first visit to the estate was during the day. They wanted to get a lay of the land and speak to residents before conducting any nighttime investigations. They introduced themselves to the community, explaining their experience and intentions. Many residents were sceptical, but others were relieved to have someone taking their experiences seriously.

The team conducted interviews with the residents who had experienced strange occurrences. They took detailed notes, looking for commonalities in the accounts. They paid particular attention to the Johnson family's experience with the message on the wall. They photographed the area where the message appeared, even though it had since vanished.

With permission from several residents, they set up surveillance equipment in and around the homes that had reported the most significant levels of activity. This included motion-sensitive cameras and audio recording devices. They planned to monitor these remotely from Jack's command centre.

Back at the command centre, the team began analysing the initial data they had collected. They approached the data with a healthy level of scepticism, looking for logical explanations like electrical faults or environmental factors that could explain the occurrences.

After the first night, the team debriefed, discussing their findings. They planned their next steps, which included more in-depth nighttime investigations, setting up more equipment, and possibly bringing in external experts, such as a historian familiar with the area and a medium

During their first night of surveillance, they observed several anomalies - unexplained cold spots, flickering lights, and one instance of a shadowy figure captured on an infrared camera. The figure appeared briefly in the Johnsons' backyard before vanishing.

3

SARAH

Next door, in house number 8, a young couple, Sarah and Tom, discussed the strange mist they had seen the previous evening. They tried to rationalize it as a natural phenomenon, but the unease in their voices was palpable. Sarah, a keen photographer, decided she would try to capture any unusual occurrences on camera. She had a keen eye for detail and a passion for capturing the beauty of everyday life. Her collection of cameras ranged from vintage film models to the latest digital SLRs. Photography was her way of documenting life's moments, a hobby she found both comforting and creatively fulfilling.

Sarah's involvement in the mystery of Hillview Gardens began innocently. During the community gathering at Emma's house, she roamed around, snapping pictures of the new neighbours, the children playing, and the general ambiance of the estate. The old oak tree, in particular, caught her attention; its ancient, twisted branches gave it a majestic yet somewhat eerie appearance, especially as the evening light cast long shadows.

That night, after hearing about the strange occurrences, Sarah decided to review her photographs. As she scrolled through the images on her digital camera, she noticed odd smudges and distortions in some of the photos. These anomalies were not present in all the pictures, but where they did appear, they seemed to have a pattern – often near the old oak tree or in the backgrounds of shots where people were gathered.

Sarah transferred the photos to her computer for a better look. She used photo editing software to zoom in and adjust the lighting and contrast. This is when she noticed more peculiarities – faint outlines of figures where there should have been none, faces in windows of houses she knew were unoccupied, and in one chilling instance, a shadowy hand reaching towards a child, just at the edge of the frame.

Remembering Mrs. Hargreaves' stories about Pendle Hill's haunted past, Sarah delved into historical photography related to the area. She found old photos of the hill and the surrounding land, some dating back to the early 20th century. Comparing these to her own, she noticed eerie similarities in the shadows and figures captured.

Feeling a mix of excitement and apprehension, Sarah shared her findings with some of the neighbours, including Emma and Jack. The images became a topic of intense discussion. Some residents were sceptical, suggesting the anomalies were just tricks of light or flaws in the camera. Others felt the photos were evidence of something supernatural at Hillview Gardens.

To get an expert opinion, Sarah reached out to a local photography club and a university professor specializing in photographic analysis. They examined her photos, acknowledging that while some anomalies could be explained by technical factors like lens flare or motion blur, others were genuinely inexplicable based on conventional photography knowledge.

Encouraged by the interest in her photographs, Sarah decided to document the estate more systematically. She set up her cameras at strategic locations, especially around the old oak tree and the houses where paranormal activity was reported. She used various techniques, including long exposure and infrared photography, to capture a wider range of phenomena.

As Sarah collected more photographic evidence, a pattern began to emerge. The anomalies appeared more frequently in photos taken at dusk or dawn, and often in areas where Mrs. Hargreaves' stories had mentioned historical witch gatherings or other supernatural occurrences.

The photographic evidence collected by Sarah added a tangible, visual dimension to the unfolding mystery of Hillview Gardens. For Sarah, the project transformed from a hobby into a personal mission, blending her artistic talents with a quest for truth. For the community, the photos served as both a source of fascination and fear, further fuelling the debate between scepticism and belief in the supernatural.

4

THE COMMUNITY MEETING

Meanwhile, at the far end of the estate, near the wooded area, an elderly resident named Mrs. Hargreaves, who had lived in the area long before the estate was built, watched the newcomers with a knowing look. Mrs. Hargreaves, an octogenarian with deep roots in the Pendle area, became an inadvertent central figure in the Hillview Gardens community.

She had stories about Pendle Hill, stories that had been passed down through generations, stories that spoke of the witches and their tragic fates. Mrs. Hargreaves knew that some pasts never truly die; they just lie dormant, waiting for the right moment to resurface.

As dusk approached, Emma organized a small get-together in her backyard, hoping to foster a sense of community. The gathering started off cheerfully, with neighbours introducing themselves and children playing around the oak tree. However, as the sky darkened, the atmosphere shifted.

The lights around the estate flickered more violently than the night before, casting elongated shadows that seemed to dance and twist unnaturally. A cold breeze swept through the gathering, causing the guests to draw closer together. The laughter and chatter died down, replaced by an oppressive silence that seemed to descend from the hill itself.

Then, without warning, the children stopped playing and stared towards the woods at the edge of the estate. Their eyes were wide, their expressions a mix of fear and fascination. They claimed to see figures moving in the shadows, figures that whispered and called out to them in voices like the rustling of leaves.

The adults quickly dismissed these claims as products of overactive imaginations, but the seed of fear had been planted. As the families retreated to their homes, the feeling of being watched, of being not quite alone, grew stronger.

In the dead of night, a piercing scream shattered the silence of Hillview Gardens. It came from house number 15, where a family had found their living room in disarray, as if a whirlwind had passed through it. The mysterious message on the wall in house number 15 became a focal point of intrigue and fear. The Johnson family, who discovered it, were the newest residents of Hillview Gardens. Their dream of a peaceful life in the suburbs was shattered in one night. The living room, where the message appeared, was previously cheerful and inviting, adorned with family photos and bright, cozy furnishings. Now, it felt tainted, its warmth replaced by an ominous chill.

The message was discovered by the youngest Johnson, Lily, who had woken up for a glass of water. Her scream upon seeing the glowing script brought the entire family, and soon after, several neighbours, to the scene. The eerie glow of the writing cast a spectral light in the room, illuminating the shocked faces of the onlookers. The script was unlike anything they had seen - it seemed ancient, its characters twisted and almost alive, pulsating with a ghostly luminescence.

Emma, from across the street, was among the first to arrive. Her interest in local history gave her an insight that others lacked. She recognized the script as reminiscent of historical accounts she'd read about witch trials and arcane rituals. Jack, the retired police officer, methodically documented the scene, taking photos and making notes, his mind racing to connect this event with his knowledge of criminal patterns.

The script, though indecipherable to the residents, had a deep cultural and historical significance. It resembled writings from the 17th century, potentially linked to the witches of Pendle Hill. Such scripts were often associated with spells, curses, and communication with otherworldly entities. The glowing nature of the script suggested an otherworldly origin, adding a layer of supernatural mystery to the event.

Realizing the need for expert opinion, Jack contacted a local historian specializing in the Pendle Witch Trials and an expert in ancient scripts. Their visit to the site brought a blend of scientific analysis and historical knowledge. The historian suggested that the script might be a form of old English mixed with symbolic runes, possibly used in witchcraft practices.

The appearance of the message became the talk of the estate. Some residents felt it was a prank, while others were convinced of its supernatural origin. This event marked a turning point in the community's perception of their new homes. The initial dismissal of the paranormal was now replaced by a growing sense of fear and curiosity.

Jack enlisted the help of a local university's linguistics department to analyse the script digitally. They used software to enhance the images, hoping to decode the message. This modern approach to an ancient mystery added a compelling contrast to the story.

The local medium, Sienna, brought in by a concerned neighbour, felt a strong energy emanating from the message. She conducted a session in the living room, claiming to sense the presence of distressed spirits. Her interpretation was that the message was a warning or a plea from the witches of Pendle Hill, though she couldn't decipher its exact meaning.

As dawn approached, the message began to fade, much to the astonishment of those present. By sunrise, it had vanished completely, leaving no trace on the wall. This transient nature of the message added to its mystique, suggesting that its appearance was tied to the night and shadows of Pendle Hill.

The disappearance of the message left more questions than answers. The Johnsons were left to grapple with the reality of living in a house that had been the focal point of a supernatural event. The rest of the community was divided between scepticism and belief, with everyone keeping a wary eye on the walls of their own homes as night fell.

Following the discovery of the mysterious message, the residents of Hillview Gardens reacted in a variety of ways, reflecting a spectrum of beliefs, fears, and scepticism. The morning after the incident, the estate was abuzz with conversations and theories. A spontaneous meeting was organized at the estate's community centre. People gathered, some out of curiosity, others due to genuine concern. The room was filled with a mix of apprehension and excitement. The air was thick with the murmur of voices as residents exchanged stories and personal experiences from the previous night.

Among the crowd, different perspectives emerged. Some residents, like Emma, were intrigued by the historical and supernatural implications. Others, including a few sceptics like Tom, viewed the event as an elaborate hoax or prank. Yet, a few, particularly the elderly and those with a penchant for the supernatural, felt a deep sense of unease, suggesting that the message was a bad omen.

Word about the incident quickly spread beyond the estate. Residents took to social media, posting photos and theories about the message. Local news outlets picked up the story, adding a layer of sensationalism. This external attention began to shape the community's perception, with some residents feeling uneasy about the unwanted fame.

5

MRS HARGREAVES

A group of local history enthusiasts, including Mrs. Hargreaves, provided context to the discussion by sharing tales and folklore of Pendle Hill's witches. Mrs Hargreaves, known for her wealth of local knowledge, she sat in her well-worn armchair, a fixture at the community centre, surrounded by an audience of fascinated residents. Her age-lined face, framed by silver hair, seemed to light up as she delved into her stories, her voice a blend of nostalgia and ominous undertone. The setting for Mrs. Hargreaves' storytelling was almost cinematic - dim lighting in the community centre's meeting room, with residents huddled around, hanging onto her every word. Outside, the wind howled, adding a natural soundtrack that heightened the eerie atmosphere.

Mrs. Hargreaves' stories were a mix of historical facts and local legends. She spoke of the infamous Pendle Witch Trials of 1612, where twelve local people were accused of witchcraft and ten were hanged. Her tales were vivid, recounting details of the trials, the superstitions that fuelled the witch hunts, and the tragic fates of those accused. She shared her personal connection to the history - her own ancestors had lived in the area during the time of the witch trials. This personal tie lent authenticity and emotional weight to her stories, making them more impactful for her audience.

Mrs. Hargreaves also delved into folklore surrounding Pendle Hill. She told of old superstitions, like the belief that witches gathered on the hill during Sabbaths, and legends of ghostly processions seen in the dead of night. Her stories were peppered with details of traditional herbal remedies, some benign, others with a darker connotation linked to witchcraft. Her storytelling was interactive; she encouraged questions and shared old books and articles she had collected over the years. She showed weathered photographs of Pendle Hill, some dating back to the early 20th century, which seemed to capture shadows and shapes that defied explanation.

One of her most captivating tales was about the old oak tree in the centre of the estate. She claimed it was known as the "Witches' Meeting Point" and was believed to be cursed. According to legend, the spirits of the Pendle witches were bound to the tree, awaiting release or revenge. Mrs. Hargreaves ended her session with a chilling story about a curse the witches had supposedly cast before their execution, vowing that their spirits would return to haunt the descendants of those who wronged them. This tale resonated deeply with the residents, especially given the recent strange occurrences.

The impact of Mrs. Hargreaves' stories on the community was profound. While some residents were sceptical, dismissing them as old wives' tales, others felt a deep sense of foreboding. Her tales added layers of historical and cultural context to the ongoing mystery, shaping the community's perception of the events unfolding around them. Mrs. Hargreaves was not just a storyteller; she was a guardian of history. Her tales preserved the memory of the Pendle witches, keeping alive the lessons of the past - about fear, injustice, and the power of belief.

6

COMMUNITY WATCH GROUPS

A sense of fear began to take root among some families. Discussions about installing additional security systems and outdoor lighting were common. Parents were more vigilant about their children, warning them not to stray far from home, especially at night.

Led by proactive residents like Jack, community watch groups were formed. These groups patrolled the estate, especially around the areas where strange occurrences were reported. Their presence was both reassuring and a constant reminder of the unease that now permeated the estate. Diverse cultural and spiritual beliefs among the residents influenced their reactions. Some turned to religious symbols and prayers for protection, while others consulted spiritual healers or psychics for guidance. This variety showcased the multicultural fabric of the community and how different cultures react to unexplained phenomena.

Regular meetings were held in the community centre, providing a platform for residents to voice their concerns and share experiences. These forums became a melting pot of ideas, fears, and speculations, fostering a sense of community, albeit one brought together by shared apprehension. The incident began to affect the daily life in Hillview Gardens. Children's outdoor playtimes were reduced, social gatherings were tinged with discussions of the paranormal, and the overall atmosphere of the estate changed from cheerful to cautious.

The ongoing mystery and fear began to take a psychological toll on some residents. Sleep disturbances, anxiety, and paranoia were reported, with some people seeking counselling. The once peaceful estate was now shrouded in an air of suspense and unease.

7

THE CHILDREN'S PERSPECTIVES

The children of Hillview Gardens, with their unfiltered views and vivid imaginations, played a unique role in the unfolding mystery. Their experiences and interpretations offered a fresh, often overlooked perspective on the strange occurrences. They were the first to notice subtle changes, like the way the wind seemed to whisper around the old oak tree or how the shadows seemed to play tricks in the fading light.

One of the first notable incidents involving the children occurred at the playground near the oak tree. A group of children, ranging in ages from five to twelve, suddenly stopped their play and stood staring at the tree, as if transfixed. They later described seeing "shadowy figures" dancing around the tree and hearing faint laughter that didn't sound like it belonged to any of them.

Following this incident, several children began to draw pictures of what they saw and heard. Their drawings were filled with curious details - figures with elongated limbs, faces hidden in the tree bark, and eyes in the shadows. Some parents dismissed these as products of active imaginations, but others were unsettled by the consistency in the children's descriptions.

A particularly eerie development was the children's accounts of night-time whispers. Several children, from different families, reported hearing their names being called softly from outside their windows late at night. These whispers enticed them with promises of secrets and hidden treasures of the hill. Parents were alarmed, resulting in a community-wide directive to keep windows closed and locked at night.

A recurring character in the children's accounts was an imaginary friend they collectively named "Maggie". According to the children, Maggie was a young girl who claimed to be from a long time ago and spoke in an old-fashioned way. Maggie seemed to know a lot about the history of Pendle Hill and the witches. Her stories, as recounted by the children, often mirrored the tales Mrs. Hargreaves shared, though with a childlike twist.

Several children began reporting similar dreams featuring the Pendle Hill witches, the oak tree, and sometimes hidden underground passages. These dreams were vivid and often shared similar themes, such as searching for something lost or being chased by an unseen force. The ongoing events began to impact the children's behaviour. Some became more withdrawn, others had trouble sleeping, and a few started exhibiting an unusual interest in historical and occult books, far beyond their usual age-appropriate interests.

At the local school, teachers reported changes in classroom dynamics. History lessons about local folklore became surprisingly engaging for students, who shared their own stories and experiences at home. Some teachers used this as an opportunity to educate the children about folklore versus reality, while others were more cautious, not wanting to fuel their fears.

Parents' reactions varied widely. Some were proactive, organizing group meetings to discuss how to handle the children's stories and experiences. Others preferred to avoid discussing the matter, fearing it would only scare the children more. This divergence in parenting styles led to some tension within the community.

Ultimately, the children's perspectives acted as a catalyst for the community. Their experiences were too consistent and alarming to ignore, leading to the increased involvement of the RIP Squad and other external investigators. The children's accounts added a layer of urgency to the investigation, as protecting them became a unifying concern for the residents of Hillview Gardens.

8

THE OAK TREE'S SIGNIFICANCE

The old oak tree, standing tall in the heart of Hillview Gardens, was more than just a natural landmark. It had an imposing presence, with gnarled branches that seemed to reach outwards like twisted fingers. Its thick trunk bore the marks of time, and its roots sprawled deep and wide into the earth. The tree was an integral part of the estate's landscape, visible from nearly every home and often the focal point for children playing.

According to Mrs. Hargreaves' tales and local folklore, the oak tree was historically known as the "Witches' Meeting Point." It was believed that, centuries ago, the witches of Pendle Hill gathered under this tree for their sabbaths and rituals. Legends suggested that the spirits of these witches were tied to the tree, either as a form of punishment or as a sacred bond with nature.

Residents started noticing odd natural phenomena surrounding the tree. Leaves would rustle when there was no wind, shadows beneath it seemed darker and more pronounced, and animals, particularly birds, avoided the tree, creating an eerie, silent bubble around it. On several occasions, residents reported seeing faint glows or mists around the tree, especially at twilight.

The children of the estate were particularly drawn to the oak tree. They played games around it, hid behind its massive trunk, and sometimes just sat staring up at its sprawling branches. After the initial sightings of shadowy figures and the whispers of "Maggie," the children's imaginary friend, their fascination seemed to increase, as if the tree held secrets only they could understand.

Sarah's photographic endeavours captured some of the most compelling evidence of the tree's unusual nature. Pictures taken of or near the tree often had distortions or unexplained figures. Some photos showed what appeared to be faces in the bark or strange symbols that were not visible to the naked eye.

The RIP Squad conducted various scientific tests around the tree. EMF readings were inconsistent, spiking unexpectedly. Soil samples revealed nothing unusual, but thermal imaging showed fluctuating temperatures around the tree, with no apparent natural cause.

The tree became a topic of cultural significance and debate within the community. Some viewed it as a symbol of the estate's connection to the local history and folklore. Others saw it as a menacing presence, a reminder of a dark past that was intruding into their lives. Discussions about the tree became a common occurrence at community meetings, with opinions divided between reverence, fear, and scientific curiosity.

As the story progressed and the supernatural occurrences intensified, the community, guided by Mrs. Hargreaves' knowledge and the RIP Squad's findings, decided to conduct a ceremony at the tree. This ritual, a blend of historical practices and modern spiritualism, aimed to appease the spirits of the witches and unravel the mysteries tied to the tree.

During the ritual, several participants reported experiencing visions and sensations that suggested the tree was more than just a physical entity; it was a gateway or conduit to another realm or a bridge between the past and present. These experiences further cemented the tree's significance in the unfolding events at Hillview Gardens.

The oak tree's significance in the narrative extended beyond its physical presence. It symbolized the deep roots of history, the intertwining of reality and legend, and the thin veil between the natural and supernatural worlds. Its legacy in the story of Hillview Gardens became a testament to the enduring power of folklore and the mysteries of the natural world.

9

THE SHADOW OF JEREMIAH COOPER

The night air was cool and still as the members of the RIP Squad assembled in Jack's garage, now transformed into their makeshift command centre. The room was dimly lit, casting long shadows over the walls lined with bookshelves and maps. Monitors displaying live feeds from various cameras around the estate flickered in the semi-darkness, creating an atmosphere that was both high-tech and eerily reminiscent of a detective's office from a bygone era.

Jack, a tall figure with a commanding presence even in retirement, stood at the head of the room. His eyes, once accustomed to scrutinizing crime scenes, now scanned the data collected from their latest foray into the supernatural. Around him, the other members of the RIP Squad gathered, each carrying a sense of urgency that was uncharacteristic of their usual hobbyist enthusiasm. Jack's journey into law enforcement began in his early twenties, driven by a deep-rooted sense of justice and a desire to make a tangible difference in his community. His initial years were marked by rigorous training and a rapid acclimatization to the demands and challenges of police work.

Known for his sharp intellect, keen observational skills, and unwavering integrity, Jack quickly rose through the ranks. He garnered respect from his colleagues and superiors alike, often being assigned to high-profile cases due to his exceptional problem-solving abilities and his knack for understanding complex criminal psychologies. Jack found his true calling as a detective. He had a talent for piecing together seemingly unrelated bits of evidence to form a coherent picture. His approach to solving cases was methodical and thorough, earning him a reputation as one of the most reliable detectives in the force.

Throughout his career, Jack worked on a variety of cases, ranging from burglary and fraud to more serious crimes like homicide. One of his most notable cases involved unravelling a complex fraud scheme that led to the arrest of several high-profile individuals in the community. In the latter part of his career, Jack took on a role that involved training and mentoring younger officers. He was passionate about passing on his knowledge and experience, shaping the next generation of law enforcement officers.

Jack retired from the police force with honours, leaving behind a legacy of dedication and excellence. However, retirement was not the end of his journey. His innate curiosity and desire to help others led him to form the RIP Squad, where he applied his investigative skills to unravelling paranormal mysteries in Hillview Gardens.

Sarah, the youngest of the group, was setting up her laptop, ready to show the latest batch of photographs she had taken around the estate. Her hands trembled slightly, a mix of fear and excitement at what she had captured on camera. Sarah grew up in a small town not far from Hillview Gardens, where she developed a keen interest in photography and storytelling from a young age. This interest was nurtured through her schooling years, where she excelled in arts and visual media. Her childhood was marked by a curious nature and a vivid imagination, traits that would serve her well in her future endeavours.

Following her passion, Sarah pursued a degree in Visual Arts, with a specialization in Photography. She was particularly fascinated by the power of images to capture and tell stories, to reveal truths that were not immediately apparent to the naked eye. Her talent and eye for detail were evident in her work, which often explored the intersection of reality and perception. After completing her education, Sarah embarked on a career as a freelance photographer. She worked on various assignments, from local events and portraits to more artistic projects. Her photography often featured elements of the unusual and the overlooked, showcasing her ability to see the extraordinary in the ordinary.

Sarah's interest in the paranormal began as a personal project. She started documenting old buildings and historical sites, drawn to their hidden histories and untold stories. It was during this time that she encountered her first unexplained phenomenon – a series of photographs that captured what appeared to be ghostly apparitions in an abandoned mansion.

Her experience with the paranormal photography piqued her interest further, leading her to research and explore more about the subject. It was this journey that eventually led her to cross paths with Jack and the other members of the RIP Squad. Recognizing her unique talents and shared interests, they invited her to join the team. In the RIP Squad, Sarah's role extended beyond just documenting their investigations. Her skills in photography became essential in capturing evidence of paranormal activity. She also brought a creative and analytical perspective to the team, often helping to piece together clues and patterns that others might overlook.

Throughout her time with the RIP Squad, Sarah's initial fascination with the paranormal evolved into a deeper understanding of the complexities of such phenomena. Her contributions to the team's investigations were not just technical but also emotional, as she often connected with the human stories behind each haunting.

Mason, a former detective with an analytical mind, was poring over a map of Hillview Gardens, marking the locations of reported paranormal incidents. His brow was furrowed, a clear sign of his deep concentration and the seriousness of their situation. Mason was born and raised in the vicinity of Ipswich, a town with a rich football heritage. From a young age, he was captivated by the sport, spending his weekends either playing in local fields or cheering on Ipswich Town Football Club, the team he grew up supporting. His enthusiasm for football was not just about the game; it was a way for him to connect with his community and family, forming a crucial part of his identity.

Mason's academic journey was marked by a keen interest in the sciences and mathematics. He excelled in logical reasoning and problem-solving, skills that he would later apply in his professional life. After completing his education, Mason pursued a career that involved data analysis in the Police, where he could utilize his analytical skills to decipher complex information patterns before applying to join the Force and eventually using his analytical skills when he became a detective.

Throughout his career, Mason found ways to intertwine his love for football with his professional skills. He was known for his statistical analyses of football games, often providing insightful breakdowns of Ipswich Town's performances. His ability to analyse patterns and predict outcomes made him a popular figure among local football enthusiasts.

Mason's personal life revolved around his family, friends, and football. He was actively involved in his community, often volunteering for events related to sports and youth programs. His commitment to his hometown was evident in everything he did, from participating in local fundraisers to coaching junior football teams. Mason's interest in the paranormal was initially sparked by a conversation at a local pub after an Ipswich Town match. A discussion about local legends and ghost stories piqued his curiosity, leading him to explore more about the subject. His analytical mind found the unexplained phenomena intriguing, and he began to apply his data analysis skills to study reported hauntings and sightings.

It was this newfound interest, after he retired, that led Mason to cross paths with Jack and the other members of the RIP Squad. They were impressed by his logical approach to paranormal investigations and his ability to remain level-headed in the face of unexplainable events. His skills in data analysis and pattern recognition made him an invaluable asset to the team. In the RIP Squad, Mason's role was multifaceted. He was instrumental in planning their investigations, analysing evidence, and developing strategies. His pragmatic approach often provided a counterbalance to the more intuitive methods of other team members. Even in the realm of the paranormal, Mason never lost touch with his passion for football. He would often be seen wearing his Ipswich Town scarf during investigations, a personal talisman and a reminder of his roots. His stories about football often served to lighten the mood, bringing a sense of normalcy to the often tense atmosphere of their investigations.

Linda, who had spent her career in forensics, was carefully organizing the evidence they had gathered - EMF readings, audio recordings, and notes from their interviews with the residents. Her methodical approach brought a semblance of order to the chaos of the unknown. Linda pursued this passion through her academic career, earning a degree in Forensic Science. Her education was comprehensive, covering various aspects of forensics, from crime scene investigation to laboratory analysis. She excelled in her studies, particularly in courses related to trace evidence and DNA analysis.

After graduating, Linda began working in a forensic laboratory. Her job involved analysing evidence collected from crime scenes, which often included working closely with law enforcement agencies. Her meticulous work helped solve numerous cases, earning her a reputation for reliability and precision. Linda specialized in trace evidence, which involves analysing small, often microscopic, materials found at crime scenes. This specialization required a keen eye and a methodical approach, both of which Linda possessed in abundance. Her ability to link minute pieces of evidence to the bigger picture was a skill that proved invaluable in her forensic work.

Linda's transition from conventional forensics to paranormal investigation was driven by her encounter with the RIP Squad. She was initially sceptical about the existence of paranormal phenomena. However, her curiosity and love for solving mysteries led her to assist the team in a case involving unexplained occurrences in Hillview Gardens. In the RIP Squad, Linda quickly became an essential member. Her forensic expertise allowed her to approach paranormal investigations with a unique perspective. She applied her skills in evidence analysis to decipher clues that others might overlook, treating each case with the same rigor as she would a crime scene.

Linda's contributions went beyond her forensic expertise. Her logical and systematic approach to problem-solving helped the team develop more structured investigation methods. She also played a key role in documenting and cataloguing the evidence they collected, ensuring that their findings were recorded with scientific precision. Linda's journey with the RIP Squad marked significant personal growth. Her initial scepticism gradually transformed into an open-mindedness towards the unexplained. She learned to balance her scientific background with the less tangible aspects of paranormal investigation, embracing the unknown while maintaining her commitment to empirical evidence.

The final member, Theo, a retired beat cop with a knack for technology, was monitoring the live feeds, keeping an eye out for any unusual activity. His once sceptical attitude had gradually given way to a reluctant acceptance of the unexplainable events they were investigating. Theo's journey began on the streets as a beat cop. He was known for his dedication and his ability to connect with the community. His time on the force was marked by a strong sense of duty and a down-to-earth approach to problem-solving. He walked his beat with a keen eye, always ready to lend a helping hand or defuse a situation with his easy-going manner.

While Theo's primary career was in law enforcement, he always had a passion for technology. He was largely self-taught, spending his free time tinkering with electronics, assembling computers, and exploring the latest gadgets. His home was often filled with parts of disassembled devices, each a project in progress or a puzzle to be solved. Theo found ways to integrate his love for technology into his police work. He was often the go-to person in his precinct for anything tech-related, from setting up computer networks to troubleshooting equipment. His superiors recognized his dual talent, and he occasionally led initiatives to introduce new technology to improve police work.

Upon retiring from the police force, Theo found himself missing the excitement and sense of purpose that came with the job. However, he also saw it as an opportunity to delve deeper into his technological interests. He started taking on small projects, helping friends and local businesses with tech setups and repairs. Theo's path crossed with the RIP Squad rather serendipitously. He met them during an investigation where they were struggling with a piece of malfunctioning equipment. With his practical know-how, Theo quickly fixed the issue, impressing the team. Intrigued by the challenge and the novel application of his skills, he accepted their invitation to join the squad.

As a member of the RIP Squad, Theo brought a unique perspective. His police training provided him with investigative skills and an understanding of procedural work, while his tech-savviness allowed the team to employ more advanced methods in their investigations. He was instrumental in setting up their equipment, ensuring everything ran smoothly during investigations, and often came up with creative tech-based solutions to paranormal challenges.

Theo's journey with the RIP Squad marked a new chapter in his life. He found a renewed sense of purpose, combining his law enforcement background with his passion for technology. His ability to stay calm under pressure and his practical approach to problem-solving made him an invaluable member of the team.

As the team settled in, Jack cleared his throat, drawing everyone's attention. "We've all seen things that challenge our understanding of the world," he began, his voice steady but tinged with concern. "But what we've discovered today might be the key to understanding what's happening in Hillview Gardens."

He motioned for Sarah to start her presentation. As the images flashed onto the screen, the room fell into a hushed silence. Each photograph displayed anomalies that defied logical explanation - shadowy figures, ghostly apparitions, and one particularly chilling image of what appeared to be a face twisted in anger and sorrow.

"It's not just the witches of Pendle we're dealing with," Jack continued, his gaze locking with each member of the team. "There's something else, a presence that's far more malevolent. We've uncovered records of a man named Jeremiah Cooper, a witchfinder's assistant from the 1600s, known for his ruthless methods. It seems his spirit is still here, trapped by guilt and a twisted sense of justice."

The revelation hung heavily in the room, a palpable sense of unease settling over the team. They knew that what they were dealing with was no longer just a curiosity, but a dangerous entity that threatened the peace and safety of Hillview Gardens.

"We need to figure out what Cooper wants and how to stop him," Jack declared, a determined look in his eyes. "This has gone beyond mere investigation. We're the only ones who can put an end to this."

The team nodded in agreement, each feeling the weight of responsibility on their shoulders. They were no longer just retired professionals chasing a hobby; they had become the guardians standing between the living and the unrestful spirits of the past.

As they delved deeper into their planning, the night outside crept on, the shadows around Hillview Gardens seeming to grow darker and more ominous, as if echoing the newfound gravity of their mission.

In the hushed, tense atmosphere of the command centre, the RIP Squad turned their attention to the historical records that lay scattered across the main table. Amidst the ancient texts and digital printouts, one name had begun to stand out with a chilling clarity - Jeremiah Cooper.

Mason, with his detective's knack for connecting the dots, had been the first to stumble upon this forgotten figure from the dark chapters of Pendle's past. He had spent hours in the local archives, poring over musty documents and old trial records, piecing together a narrative that had long been buried under the dust of time.

"Jeremiah Cooper wasn't just any witchfinder's assistant," Mason began, his voice a sombre echo in the room. "He was notorious for his cruelty and zealotry. Records show that he took a perverse pleasure in hunting those accused of witchcraft, often inventing evidence to ensure their conviction."

The team listened, rapt, as Mason unfolded the tale. Jeremiah Cooper had been a young man during the height of the Pendle Witch Trials, a period marked by fear and superstition. He had worked under the infamous witchfinder John Kincaid, a man known for his brutal methods of extracting confessions from the accused.

But there was more to Jeremiah's story than just his cruel deeds. Mason had found a series of journal entries, believed to be written by Jeremiah himself, in the latter years of his life. These entries painted the picture of a man tormented by guilt and doubt.

"He started questioning the convictions, wondering if those he helped condemn were actually innocent," Mason explained, holding up a reproduction of one of the journal pages. The handwriting was cramped and erratic, the words of a man wrestling with his conscience.

Linda, leaning over the journal, added, "It seems like his guilt followed him to his grave. According to local lore, he died under mysterious circumstances, and his burial site was never recorded. It's as if he vanished from history."

Jack, connecting the dots, said, "So, we're dealing with a spirit that's not just trapped but is fuelled by guilt and a twisted sense of unfinished business. He's trying to capture the souls of the witches' descendants, thinking he's still serving justice."

The revelation cast a new light on the strange occurrences at Hillview Gardens. The malevolent activities, the aggressive nature of the hauntings - it all pointed to a spirit that was not just lingering but actively pursuing a misguided mission from centuries ago.

Sarah, who had been silently absorbing the discussion, spoke up, "The photo I took near the oak tree, the one with the face full of anger and sorrow... could that be Jeremiah?"

The team turned to look at the photograph again, the spectral image now taking on a new, more ominous meaning. The face in the photo did seem to resonate with the tragic tale of Jeremiah Cooper - a man who, in his quest for redemption, had become something far more sinister.

As the team sat in contemplative silence, the weight of history pressing in around them, they realized that they were not just facing the echoes of a bygone era. They were confronting a deeply troubled soul, one that had been festering in the shadows of Pendle Hill for centuries, waiting for a chance to right the wrongs he had committed, no matter the cost.

In the dim light of Jack's command centre, the RIP Squad gathered around as Mason unfurled the yellowed pages of an ancient journal, the supposed writings of Jeremiah Cooper. The pages were delicate, the ink faded but still legible, bearing the testimony of a tormented soul.

The entries, dating back to the late 1600s, began with mundane observations but gradually descended into a maelstrom of guilt and fear. Jeremiah's words were scrawled in a hurried hand, the script becoming more erratic as his confessions grew more frantic.

"He writes of nightmares, visions of the women he helped condemn," Mason read aloud, his voice echoing the despair in Jeremiah's words. "He talks about hearing their cries, seeing their faces in his dreams, accusing him of their unjust deaths."

The entries painted a portrait of a man haunted by his past actions. Jeremiah's initial unwavering belief in the righteousness of his mission had crumbled, leaving him to grapple with the reality of his role in the tragic fate of innocent lives.

Linda, examining the journal, pointed out a particularly harrowing entry. "Here, he speaks of trying to make amends, seeking out the families of those he wronged, but being shunned and cursed by them. He was a pariah, haunted by both the living and the dead."

The team fell into a contemplative silence, each member processing the tragic irony of Jeremiah's plight. His quest for redemption had only deepened his torment, both in life and, it seemed, in death as well.

"It's as if his guilt has anchored his spirit to this world," Jack mused, his brow furrowed in thought. "He's trapped in a loop of his own making, trying to capture the souls of the witches and their descendants, believing it's his path to salvation."

Sarah, still haunted by the image she captured near the oak tree, added softly, "Maybe that's why the activity here is so aggressive. Jeremiah's spirit doesn't just linger; it acts with purpose, driven by a twisted notion of justice."

Theo, who had been quietly listening, chimed in, "It's like he's still playing the role of the witchfinder's assistant, hunting and tormenting, unable to let go of his perceived duty."

The realization dawned on the team that they were not just dealing with a restless ghost, but with a spirit consumed by guilt and a misguided sense of obligation. Jeremiah Cooper, in his pursuit of redemption, had become a malevolent force, his actions in the afterlife mirroring the zealotry and cruelty that had marked his time as a witchfinder's assistant.

As the team delved deeper into the journal, the entries became more disjointed, a clear sign of Jeremiah's deteriorating mental state. His final entries were a mix of pleas for forgiveness and declarations of a continued mission, a chilling testament to the depth of his delusion and despair.

As the RIP Squad delved deeper into the tragic tale of Jeremiah Cooper, a noticeable surge in paranormal activity began to grip Hillview Gardens. The once peaceful estate was now a hotbed of unexplained phenomena, with each incident seemingly more intense than the last.

In the quiet of the night, the residents started reporting a series of disturbing occurrences. Kitchen utensils would rattle inexplicably, heavy footsteps echoed in empty hallways, and doors slammed shut with no apparent cause. One family awoke to find their living room furniture rearranged in a bizarre, almost ritualistic, pattern.

Cold spots began to appear throughout the estate, sudden drops in temperature that defied logical explanation. These frigid zones would materialize randomly, leaving residents shivering and breathless. In one instance, a visible frost formed on the interior of a home's windows, despite the heating system working overtime.

More alarming were the reports of physical contact. Several residents experienced the sensation of being touched, grabbed, or even pushed by unseen hands. A young mother recounted feeling a forceful tug on her hair while doing laundry in her basement, turning around to find no one there.

Objects moving on their own became a common occurrence. Books would fly off shelves, pictures would fall off walls, and children's toys would move across the floor unaided. One particularly unsettling incident involved a set of kitchen knives being found embedded in the wooden floor of the dining area.

The wind seemed to carry whispers, unintelligible murmurs that sent shivers down the spines of those who heard them. These whispers often seemed to emanate from the direction of the old oak tree, adding to the tree's already eerie reputation.

Shadows began to play tricks on the eyes of the residents. What appeared to be normal shadows cast by objects would morph and twist, creating unsettling shapes and figures. Some claimed to see the silhouette of a man, tall and thin, looming ominously before dissipating into the darkness.

The escalation in activity brought a heightened sense of fear and anxiety to the community. Sleep became elusive for many residents, and the once friendly and open conversations turned to hushed, nervous discussions about leaving Hillview Gardens.

The RIP Squad, utilizing their surveillance equipment, captured much of this activity. The monitors in their command centre were now filled with real-time evidence of the haunting - chilling footage that corroborated the residents' accounts. The team worked tirelessly, documenting and trying to find patterns in the activity.

Amidst all these occurrences, there was a palpable sense of a presence, an unseen entity that was orchestrating these events. The feeling of being watched, of being hunted, became a constant companion to the residents, casting a shadow over the once idyllic estate.

10

SARAH'S CHILLING ENCOUNTER

The evening had settled over Hillview Gardens with a quiet, unnerving calm. Sarah, armed with her camera, ventured out to capture more of the inexplicable phenomena that were increasingly plaguing the estate. Her steps were cautious, her eyes constantly scanning the dimly lit surroundings. The air was thick with a sense of foreboding, and every rustle of leaves sent her heart racing.

Determined to document the paranormal occurrences, Sarah decided to focus on the old oak tree. Its gnarled branches and sprawling roots had become the epicentre of many chilling tales from the residents. As she approached, the air around her seemed to grow colder, the atmosphere denser.

Setting up her tripod, Sarah adjusted her camera settings for night photography. Through her viewfinder, the tree appeared more ominous than ever. She snapped a few pictures, then paused, feeling an inexplicable pull to look closer at the tree's trunk.

As she zoomed in, Sarah's breath caught in her throat. There, in the camera's display, was the faint outline of a figure, barely discernible against the bark of the tree. It appeared to be a man, tall and gaunt, his face contorted in what seemed like anguish and rage. The figure was not visible to the naked eye, only through the lens of her camera.

With a mix of fear and fascination, Sarah continued to photograph the apparition. The figure seemed to become clearer with each click of the shutter, its features growing more defined, more menacing. It was as if her camera had pierced a veil into another realm, revealing the tormented spirit of Jeremiah Cooper.

The air around Sarah grew chillingly cold, her breath forming visible puffs in the night air. She could feel an oppressive energy emanating from the figure in her camera, a sense of deep sorrow mixed with malevolent intent. It was as though Jeremiah's spirit was reaching out from the photograph, its emotions palpable and overwhelming.

Overcome with fear, Sarah quickly packed up her equipment and hurried back to the safety of her home. Her mind was racing, trying to process what she had just witnessed. The encounter had been terrifyingly intimate, a direct confrontation with the restless spirit they were investigating.

Back in her home, Sarah uploaded the photographs to her computer. The image of the apparition was even more striking on the larger screen. The face of Jeremiah Cooper, if indeed it was him, was marked by centuries of guilt and rage, a spectral embodiment of the tragic tale they had uncovered.

Shaken, Sarah immediately contacted Jack and the rest of the RIP Squad, sharing the photographs with them. The team was equally stunned. The images were the most compelling evidence yet of the supernatural forces at play in Hillview Gardens. They were not just dealing with random hauntings; they were facing a spirit with a history, a purpose, and a chilling presence.

11

THE CHILDREN'S DISTURBED SLEEP

As the haunting of Hillview Gardens escalated, its youngest residents began to bear the brunt of its eerie manifestations. The children, once full of laughter and playful energy, now faced nights filled with terror and unrest.

The change first became apparent when several children started reporting strikingly similar nightmares. Parents across the estate spoke of their children waking up in the middle of the night, crying and shaking with fear. These were not ordinary bad dreams; they were vivid and hauntingly consistent among the children.

In hushed conversations at bus stops and over backyard fences, parents shared the unsettling details of these nightmares. The children spoke of a 'scary man' who lurked in the shadows of their rooms, his eyes like burning coals, his whispers cold and menacing. Some recounted being chased through endless, dark corridors, feeling an overwhelming sense of dread.

The descriptions of the 'scary man' bore a chilling resemblance to the historical figure of Jeremiah Cooper. His tall, gaunt appearance matched the apparition captured in Sarah's photographs, suggesting that his tormented spirit was not just haunting the physical spaces of the estate but also invading the children's dreams.

In some instances, the nightmares seemed to manifest physically. Children would wake up with unexplained scratches or bruises, or find their room in disarray, with toys and books strewn about as if caught in an unseen maelstrom. One child woke up clutching an old-fashioned locket that the parents could not account for.

Alarmed and desperate to protect their children, parents took various measures. Some turned to religious symbols, placing crosses or other protective items in their children's rooms. Others kept nightlights on or took to sleeping in their children's rooms, offering whatever comfort they could.

Seeking answers, several families consulted with child psychologists, hoping to find a rational explanation for the nightmares. At the same time, others reached out to mediums or spiritual advisors, looking for supernatural solutions to what they were coming to believe was a haunting that targeted their children.

The disturbed sleep took a toll on the children's daytime behaviour. Many became withdrawn, their playful spirits dampened by fatigue and fear. Schoolteachers reported a noticeable change in their students, with previously bright and engaged children now listless and distracted.

As these reports multiplied, the community's concern grew. Playgrounds and schoolyards, once filled with the carefree sounds of children playing, now echoed with worried conversations among parents and caregivers. The estate's atmosphere, already heavy with the adults' fears, became tinged with a more profound sense of urgency to protect its youngest and most vulnerable residents.

12

A TENSE SÉANCE

Recognizing the need for more direct contact with the spiritual forces at play, the RIP Squad decided to arrange a séance. They enlisted the help of Sienna, a locally renowned medium known for her sensitivity to paranormal phenomena. The séance was set in the living room of the Johnson family, where the first disturbing message on the wall had appeared.

Sienna arrived at dusk, dressed in flowing garments, her eyes conveying a depth of knowledge and experience. She began by preparing the room, dimming the lights and arranging a circle of chairs around a small, antique table. She placed candles at strategic points and instructed everyone to join hands.

As the candles flickered, casting dancing shadows on the walls, Sienna began to chant in a low, rhythmic tone. The air in the room grew heavier, and a sense of anticipation hung palpably among the participants. The RIP Squad members exchanged nervous glances, their scepticism momentarily suspended in the face of the unknown.

Sienna's voice grew stronger as she called out to the spirits of Hillview Gardens. "Spirits of this place, we seek your presence and understanding," she intoned. The flames of the candles seemed to respond, flickering more intensely as if swayed by an unseen breeze.

After several minutes of tense silence, a cold draft swept through the room, causing the participants to shiver. Sienna's eyes fluttered closed, and her body stiffened. In a voice not her own, deeper and laced with pain, she spoke, "I am bound... unable to find peace... guilt and duty chain me."

The atmosphere in the room shifted dramatically. Objects began to tremble; the table vibrated under the participants' hands. The medium's voice, now clearly that of a troubled male entity, continued to speak of guilt, injustice, and an unending quest for redemption. The candles blew out abruptly, plunging the room into darkness, save for the eerie glow of a single candle that remained lit before Sienna.

Amidst the chaos, a translucent figure materialized briefly near the table. It was the gaunt, anguished face of a man – presumed to be Jeremiah Cooper – his expression twisted in a grimace of sorrow and anger. The sight was fleeting, but it left the participants in no doubt of the spirit's powerful presence.

As quickly as it had begun, the séance came to an abrupt end. Sienna gasped for air, her body relaxing as she returned to her normal state. She warned the group that Jeremiah's spirit was incredibly strong and tormented, driven by a complex mix of emotions. "He is dangerous," she cautioned, "trapped in his own cycle of guilt and perceived duty. To bring peace, you must help him break free from his bonds."

The participants were left shaken by the experience. The séance had not only confirmed the presence of Jeremiah Cooper's spirit but also highlighted the depth of his turmoil. The RIP Squad now understood that they were dealing with a deeply complex and troubled entity, one that would not be easily appeased or banished.

In the aftermath of the intense séance, the participants sat in stunned silence, the air still thick with the lingering presence of Jeremiah Cooper's spirit. Sienna, her face pale and drawn from the energy expended, gathered herself to impart a crucial warning to the RIP Squad and the gathered residents.

Regaining her composure, Sienna spoke with a seriousness that commanded the room's attention. "The spirit of Jeremiah Cooper is not just lingering here; he is bound by his own tormented psyche," she explained. "His actions are fuelled by a powerful mix of guilt and a misguided sense of duty. He believes he is still serving justice, yet he is blinded by his own unresolved guilt."

She continued to detail the complexity of Jeremiah's spiritual state. Unlike many spirits who are confused or lost, Jeremiah's spirit was coherent, purposeful, and deeply troubled. His actions were not random hauntings but deliberate attempts to continue his perceived mission from centuries ago.

"The danger he poses is significant," Sienna cautioned. "His guilt has turned into a form of spiritual madness, driving him to target the descendants of those he wronged. He seeks to capture their souls, believing it to be his path to redemption."

She emphasized the need for a careful, considered approach in dealing with Jeremiah's spirit. Confronting him directly could provoke a violent reaction, as his belief in his mission had only strengthened over the centuries. Any attempt to communicate or appease him needed to acknowledge his mindset and find a way to break through his cycle of guilt and duty.

Sienna also spoke of the old oak tree, suggesting it was a focal point for Jeremiah's energy. "The tree may hold the key," she said. "It's a symbol of both the historical events and his current anchor to this world. Understanding its significance to him might be crucial in resolving this haunting."

She warned that the situation could escalate if not addressed soon. Jeremiah's spirit was growing more restless and powerful, feeding off the fear and anxiety of the residents. This escalation could lead to more dangerous and potentially harmful encounters.

Finally, Sienna stressed the importance of resolving the past. "To bring peace to Jeremiah and this community, you must help him confront and accept the truth of his actions. Only then can he be released from his self-imposed purgatory."

As the session concluded, the RIP Squad and the residents were left to ponder the weight of the task ahead. They now understood the depth of the challenge they faced – not just a haunting, but a battle against a centuries-old spirit trapped in his own nightmare of guilt and retribution.

13

DELVING INTO HISTORY FOR ANSWERS

IN THE WAKE OF SIENNA'S warning, the RIP Squad recognized the need to delve deeper into the history surrounding Jeremiah Cooper. Understanding his past was key to confronting the malevolent spirit haunting Hillview Gardens. This section of the chapter is marked by a detailed investigation, combining historical research with modern detective work.

The team began by gathering all available historical records about the Pendle Witch Trials and specifically about Jeremiah Cooper. This included visiting local archives, libraries, and even contacting historians specializing in that period. Mason, with his detective background, took the lead, meticulously sifting through old court documents, trial transcripts, and historical accounts.

A significant portion of their research focused on the journal believed to be written by Jeremiah Cooper. Linda, with her expertise in forensic analysis, examined the handwriting and paper for authenticity, confirming that the journal was indeed from the 17th century. The journal entries provided a window into Jeremiah's tormented mind, revealing his growing doubts about the guilt of those he helped condemn and his subsequent descent into madness.

The team also sought out descendants of the Pendle witches, some of whom still lived in the surrounding areas. These interviews provided personal family stories and legends passed down through generations, adding a human element to the historical facts. These stories often included mentions of Jeremiah Cooper, reinforcing his infamy and the fear he instilled even centuries later.

Understanding the folklore and legends of the time was crucial. The team visited the site of the original Pendle Witch Trials and spoke with local folklore experts. They learned about the superstitions and beliefs of the 17th century, which provided context for understanding the actions and mindset of a witchfinder's assistant.

Their research also delved into the history of the old oak tree, believed to be a meeting place for the accused witches. Historical records indicated that the tree was already ancient during Jeremiah's time, possibly used as a landmark in witch-hunting activities. This reinforced Sienna's suggestion of the tree's significance.

Combining historical data with the paranormal evidence they had gathered, the team began to piece together a timeline of Jeremiah's life and actions. They identified key events that might have triggered his guilt and his eventual transformation into a vengeful spirit.

Part of their research involved understanding the practices and beliefs of witchfinders. They studied texts from the era, learning about the methods used to identify and persecute witches. This helped them understand the mindset that drove Jeremiah to his fanatical zeal, which seemed to persist in his spectral form. The witchfinders, who emerged prominently during the witch hunts of the 16th to 18th centuries, particularly in Europe and North America, played a notorious role in the identification and persecution of individuals accused of witchcraft. Their methods and motivations were varied, often driven by a mix of religious fervour, social and political factors, and, in some cases, personal gain.

The rise of witchfinders coincided with periods of intense witch-hunting hysteria, often in regions where belief in witchcraft was widespread and where societal and religious upheavals were occurring. Witchfinders were typically self-appointed individuals who claimed to have the ability to identify witches. In some cases, they were hired by villages or towns to root out witchcraft.

Notable witchfinders included Matthew Hopkins, known as the "Witchfinder General" in England during the 17th century, and his associate John Stearne. Witchfinders often looked for physical evidence of witchcraft, known as 'witch's marks' (like moles, birthmarks, or blemishes). They believed these marks were where the devil had suckled or left his mark. A cruel and dangerous method where the accused were tied up and thrown into water. It was believed that if they floated, they were guilty of witchcraft, as the water, a pure element, was rejecting them.

The work of witchfinders often intersected with societal and economic factors. Accusations of witchcraft could be used to settle personal vendettas, seize property, or remove socially marginalized individuals. In some cases, witchfinders were paid per conviction, which incentivized the identification and conviction of witches, leading to widespread abuse and false accusations.

Witchfinders used needles or blades to prick the skin of the accused, searching for insensitive spots which were considered witch's marks. Torture was frequently used to extract confessions. Sleep deprivation, starvation, and physical pain were common methods. Accused witches were closely watched for several days. Any unusual behaviour was seen as evidence of witchcraft.

The influence of witchfinders waned as the witch trials declined. This was due to a combination of factors, including growing scepticism about the existence of witchcraft, legal reforms, and increasing awareness of the injustices and fallacies of the trials. The legacy of witchfinders remains a dark chapter in history, highlighting the dangers of superstition, the abuse of power, and mass hysteria.

Finally, the team consulted with historians and psychologists, seeking opinions on Jeremiah's psychological profile based on his journal and historical actions. According to the profile, Jeremiah was likely very dedicated to his duties, possibly driven by a strong belief in the righteousness of his cause. This could have stemmed from a deep-seated fear of the unknown or a desire to uphold societal and religious norms. Working under a witchfinder, Jeremiah might have been highly susceptible to authority, adopting and internalizing the beliefs and practices of his superiors without question. As time went on, Jeremiah possibly began to experience cognitive dissonance as he grappled with the reality of his actions versus his moral compass. This internal conflict might have led to significant psychological distress. His actions during the witch trials, especially towards innocent people, likely led to intense feelings of guilt and remorse, particularly later in his life. These emotions might have been overwhelming, leading to a deep existential crisis.

As a spirit, Jeremiah's unresolved guilt appears to have kept him anchored to the physical world. His inability to forgive himself or find redemption might have left him in a state of perpetual unrest. His actions as a ghost, particularly targeting descendants of the accused witches, suggest a repetition compulsion. This can be seen as an unconscious attempt to relive and possibly rectify his past, indicating a deep-seated need for resolution. The haunting nature of his spirit, including inducing fear and harm, could be a manifestation of his inner torment and a projection of his own fear and guilt onto others. The conclusion went on to read that Jeremiah's psychological profile reflects a complex interplay of historical context, personal beliefs, and emotional turmoil. His journey from a fervent witchfinder's assistant to a tormented spirit is marked by a struggle with guilt, morality, and a desperate search for redemption. Understanding his psychological state provides deeper insight into his actions both in life and in death, highlighting the tragic human element in his story.

This multidisciplinary approach provided a more rounded view of his character and motivations, crucial for planning their confrontation with his spirit.

14

FORMULATING A PLAN

AFTER EXTENSIVE RESEARCH and deliberation, the RIP Squad convened in Jack's command centre to formulate a plan to confront and resolve the restless spirit of Jeremiah Cooper. The atmosphere was charged with a mix of determination and apprehension. The information gathered from historical records, interviews, and paranormal investigations had provided them with a clearer picture of Jeremiah's motivations and weaknesses. Now, it was time to translate this knowledge into action.

The first step was to establish clear objectives. The primary goal was to appease Jeremiah's spirit, helping it to break free from the cycle of guilt and perceived duty. Secondary objectives included ensuring the safety of the community and preventing further paranormal disturbances.

The plan needed to be multifaceted, combining historical understanding, psychological strategies, and paranormal techniques. Linda suggested using elements from Jeremiah's time, such as symbols or phrases from the witch trials, to create a familiar context for communication.

Mason proposed a historical reenactment. By staging a symbolic trial or hearing, they could provide Jeremiah with a platform to express his guilt and seek forgiveness, potentially releasing him from his self-imposed duty. This reenactment would take place near the old oak tree, given its significance.

Sienna would play a key role in the plan. Her ability to communicate with spirits would be crucial in guiding the interaction with Jeremiah's spirit. She would also serve as a mediator, ensuring the safety of all participants.

Theo outlined the use of their paranormal equipment to monitor the event and gather evidence. This included EMF meters, thermal cameras, and audio recording devices to document any supernatural occurrences and ensure they were prepared for any unexpected developments.

Understanding the mental and emotional toll such an encounter could take, Sarah suggested sessions with a psychologist beforehand. These sessions would prepare the team and volunteers from the community for the potentially disturbing experiences of confronting a tormented spirit.

Safety was paramount. The plan included measures to quickly evacuate the area in case of dangerous paranormal activity. Jack also arranged for medical personnel to be on standby and for the local police to be informed, without revealing the true nature of the event.

The team decided to involve select members of the community, particularly those who had experienced the most significant disturbances. Their participation would provide a personal element to the reenactment, potentially strengthening its impact on Jeremiah's spirit.

Once the plan was finalized, the team reviewed every detail, anticipating possible scenarios and preparing contingencies. Sienna conducted a final briefing on dealing with spiritual entities, emphasizing respect and caution.

The date for the reenactment was set, coinciding with the anniversary of the Pendle Witch Trials, to add historical resonance. The team, though anxious about the unknown variables of their plan, felt a sense of resolve. They were about to embark on a unique confrontation, one that bridged the gap between history and the supernatural.

15

JEREMIAH COOPER

The trial of the witches unfolds in the grim, austere courtroom of Pendle, a town gripped by fear and superstition. The year is 1612, a time when the mere whisper of witchcraft could condemn one to death. The air is thick with a foreboding sense of dread, the crowd's murmurs like the rustling of dry leaves in a cold wind. The courtroom is a place of shadows and dim candlelight, casting eerie patterns on the stone walls. At the centre stands Jeremiah Cooper, his face a mask of stern conviction. Beside him, the infamous witchfinder, John Kincaid, looms like a dark Specter, his presence commanding and fearsome.

Jeremiah's eyes are alight with a fervent zeal, betraying no hint of doubt as he assists Kincaid. He moves with a purpose, his voice unwavering as he interrogates the accused, each question laced with an implicit threat of dire consequences.

The accused witches, a parade of beleaguered souls, are brought forth. Their faces are etched with fear and despair, some trembling, others wearing a facade of defiant bravery. They are mothers, daughters, healers – now labelled as agents of darkness.

Jeremiah is relentless in his interrogations, his methods chilling in their efficiency. He employs psychological tactics, twisting their words, and when that fails, he resorts to physical means – thumbscrews, the crushing of limbs, each method designed to elicit a confession, regardless of its truth.

As the trials progress, a subtle shift occurs in Jeremiah. Doubt begins to cloud his once clear vision. He starts to notice the incongruities in the confessions, the implausibility of the accusations. The fear in the eyes of the accused mirrors a growing horror within himself. The public's reaction is a mix of hysteria and silent dread. The courtroom becomes a theatre of paranoia, where neighbours denounce neighbours, and the line between truth and fabrication blurs in the frenzy of fear.

The sentences are delivered with a cold finality. The condemned witches are led away, their fates sealed. Jeremiah watches, a hollow feeling growing in his chest. The weight of their impending doom hangs heavy in the air, a tangible Specter of death. In the quiet hours of the night, Jeremiah is haunted by the faces of those he helped condemn. The realization that he may have sent innocent souls to their deaths begins to gnaw at his conscience, a relentless whisper in the dark.

The grim setting of the execution unfolds on a bleak, windswept hill just outside Pendle, the designated spot for the execution of the accused witches. The sky is a tapestry of dark, ominous clouds, as if nature itself is mourning the impending tragedy. A large, baying crowd has gathered, their faces a mix of fear, excitement, and in some cases, barely concealed horror.

Jeremiah stands apart from the crowd, his figure silhouetted against the gray sky. As he watches the condemned witches being led to the stake, a profound realization dawns upon him. The certainty that once fuelled his crusade crumbles, leaving him engulfed in doubt and horror. The faces of the accused are etched into his memory, their expressions of resigned fate and silent accusation haunting him.

As the executioner lights the pyre, the flames leap into the air, casting a hellish glow over the scene. Jeremiah's eyes are fixed on the fire, and in its flickering light, he sees the faces of those he has condemned. Their screams pierce the air, a chorus of agony and injustice that stabs at his heart.

The crowd's reactions are a stark contrast to Jeremiah's turmoil. Some shout and jeer, caught up in the frenzy of the spectacle. Others watch with sombre, troubled expressions, their silence speaking volumes of their internal conflict. Jeremiah feels a deep chasm opening between himself and the crowd, a sense of isolation that engulfs him.

As the flames rise higher, consuming the accused in a fiery maelstrom, Jeremiah's despair reaches its zenith. He stumbles backward, his mind reeling from the horrific realization of what he has been a part of. The screams of the dying witches mingle with the howling wind, creating a cacophony that seems to resonate with his soul's torment.

In a moment of overwhelming anguish, Jeremiah makes a fateful decision. He cannot live with the burden of his deeds. Tormented by visions of the innocent lives he helped destroy, he resolves to escape the unbearable guilt that has consumed him. Jeremiah walked away from the burning pyre, his figure diminishing into the distance. The scene fades with him disappearing into the dark woods surrounding Pendle, his path illuminated only by the eerie light of the distant fire. It is a poignant, haunting image – a man lost to history, but whose spirit is destined to linger, trapped in eternal torment.

In the bleak aftermath of the Pendle Witch Trials, the once fervent witchfinder's assistant, Jeremiah Cooper, found himself wandering the shadowed path of guilt and isolation. The small, dilapidated cottage that Jeremiah called home, situated on the desolate outskirts of Pendle, shrouded in a perpetual gloom, mirrored Jeremiah's tormented psyche.

The interior of the cottage was a reflection of his troubled mind. The walls were lined with frantic scrawlings, a mix of biblical verses and pleas for forgiveness. His journal lay open on a rickety wooden table, filled with ramblings of guilt and haunting revelations. At night, the howling wind seemed to carry voices, accusatory whispers that seeped through the cracks in the walls, keeping him from rest.

Jeremiah's appearance had become ghostly, his once sturdy frame now gaunt and hunched. His eyes, once sharp and accusing, now held a haunted look, constantly darting to the shadows as if expecting to see the spectres of those he had wronged. Villagers spoke of seeing him wandering the woods near Pendle Hill, often muttering to himself, a figure both pitied and feared.

In his isolation, Jeremiah's grasp on reality began to fray. He was haunted not only by nightmares but also by visions in his waking hours – apparitions of the women he had helped to condemn, their faces twisted in agony and betrayal. He started to believe that these visions were a punishment for his sins, a curse laid upon him by the very witches he had once hunted.

As the years passed, Jeremiah's search for redemption became an obsession. He would spend hours in fervent prayer, only to lapse into fits of rage, cursing his fate and the role he had played in the witch trials. His journal entries grew more disjointed, a chaotic tapestry of remorse and delusion.

The circumstances of Jeremiah's death were as mysterious as his latter years. One winter's night, after a particularly violent storm, the villagers found his cottage abandoned, the door ajar, and the hearth cold. Inside, his journal lay on the table, open to a final entry – a plea for forgiveness from the souls he had wronged. A search was conducted, but Jeremiah was nowhere to be found. It was as if he had been swallowed by the very woods he used to roam.

Centuries later, the construction of Hillview Gardens on the land steeped in the dark history of the Pendle Witch Trials stirred the dormant spirit of Jeremiah Cooper. The disturbance of the land, especially around the old oak tree, a silent sentinel to the bygone horrors, awakened his restless soul.

Jeremiah's spirit, bound by the unresolved guilt and a warped sense of duty, found itself drawn to the modern-day estate. The presence of descendants of those he had wronged centuries ago rekindled his zealotry, igniting the haunting that plagued Hillview Gardens. The oak tree, under which he had once stood in judgment, now served as a conduit for his spectral return, a link between his tormented past and the present.

As the anniversary of the trials approached, Jeremiah's spirit grew more active, more desperate in its actions. It was as if he was reliving his final days, trapped in a cycle of his own making – seeking redemption in a world he no longer belonged to, forever bound to the land that had witnessed his greatest folly.

16

SHADOWS OF THE OAK TREE

In the modern-day setting of Hillview Gardens, the community faces a chilling crisis. The chapter opens on a typical sunny afternoon, children playing in the yards, the laughter and chatter a stark contrast to the underlying tension that permeates the estate. But as the day wanes, a sense of dread descends with the twilight.

The tranquillity is shattered when a young girl, eight-year-old Emily Harris, is reported missing. She was last seen playing near the old oak tree, her favourite spot, known for its sprawling roots and gnarled branches. Her sudden disappearance sends shockwaves through the community.

Emily's parents, Laura and Michael Harris, are depicted in the throes of unimaginable anguish. Their home, once filled with the joyful noise of Emily's presence, is now suffocated by an eerie silence. Laura spends hours by the window, her eyes scanning the estate, while Michael tirelessly organizes search parties, his voice hoarse from calling out his daughter's name.

The residents of Hillview Gardens rally together in a desperate effort to find Emily. Neighbours, previously distant, come together, united by a common fear and purpose. The local community centre becomes an impromptu headquarters for the search efforts, maps of the area plastered on the walls, and volunteers coordinating efforts.

The local children, questioned by the authorities, speak of last seeing Emily playing by the oak tree, her fascination with the ancient landmark well-known among her peers. Some children hesitantly share stories of the 'scary man' they sometimes see near the tree, their descriptions chillingly reminiscent of Jeremiah Cooper.

As hours turn into days with no sign of Emily, tension escalates within the community. Theories abound, some rational – like the possibility of her getting lost in the nearby woods – and others tinged with the supernatural, fuelled by the recent hauntings and the ominous history of the oak tree.

The RIP Squad, already deeply entrenched in the mysteries of Hillview Gardens, becomes involved in the search. They use their equipment to scan the area, particularly around the oak tree, for any clues. Jack, feeling a personal responsibility, vows to leave no stone unturned.

The disappearance of Emily Harris attracts media attention, casting a spotlight on Hillview Gardens. Reporters and camera crews descend upon the estate, capturing the growing despair of the community and the frantic search efforts.

In a particularly poignant and heart-wrenching scene, Laura Harris, mother of the missing Emily, stands under the ominous boughs of the ancient oak tree. The setting is a sombre evening, with the sun setting in the background, casting long shadows across the gardens and adding a surreal, almost ethereal quality to the scene.

The residents of Hillview Gardens have gathered, forming a semi-circle around Laura. Their faces are etched with concern and empathy, reflecting the shared fear and sorrow of the community. The murmurs of the crowd quiet down as Laura steps forward, a solitary figure in the fading light.

Laura appears visibly shaken, her eyes red from crying, yet there is a determined resolve in her posture. Clutching a small teddy bear that belongs to Emily, she clears her throat, her voice trembling as she prepares to address the crowd. Michael, her husband, stands by her side, offering silent support.

With a deep breath, Laura begins to speak, her voice echoing in the quiet of the evening. "I am standing here, in Emily's favourite place, under this tree where she loved to play," she starts, her voice breaking with emotion. "Emily is a bright, kind-hearted child, and she means everything to us."

Laura takes a moment to describe Emily, painting a picture of her daughter for the gathered crowd. "She has a laugh that can light up a room and a curiosity that knows no bounds. She loves this tree, these gardens, and all the stories they hold," Laura continues, her voice gaining strength as she speaks.

Tears stream down Laura's cheeks as she holds up Emily's teddy bear. "Emily, if you can hear me, we love you, and we are doing everything we can to find you," she says, her voice a mix of desperation and love. The emotional impact on the crowd is palpable, with many residents also shedding tears, deeply moved by the raw display of a mother's love.

Laura's plea is not only directed at the residents but also at the media crews present. She turns to the cameras, her message clear and direct. "Please help us bring our daughter home. She is out there somewhere, and she needs us."

She appeals directly to the community, her gaze moving across the faces of her neighbours. "We are asking, pleading, for any information that might help us find our little girl. If anyone saw anything, no matter how small or insignificant it may seem, please come forward."

As Laura finishes her plea, the crowd erupts in a chorus of supportive shouts and promises to help. The sense of community is strong, with neighbours vowing to continue the search and keep an eye out for any signs of Emily.

The scene concludes with the residents lighting candles around the base of the oak tree, creating a vigil for Emily. The flickering candles cast a soft glow, symbolizing hope in the midst of darkness. Laura and Michael stand together, holding hands, surrounded by their community, united in their hope and determination to find their daughter.

17

A PROMISING LEAD

As the candles flickered in the growing darkness at the base of the ancient oak tree, a solemn Jack stood apart from the gathered crowd, his gaze fixed on the gnarled bark and sprawling roots. The poignant scene of Laura's plea echoed in his mind, amplifying a suspicion that had been growing within him – that the disappearance of young Emily Harris was intertwined with the haunting Specter Jack, with years of experience in law enforcement, was no stranger to the heartache of missing persons cases. Yet, this situation was different. The recent surge in paranormal activity at Hillview Gardens, particularly surrounding the old oak tree, suggested a more sinister dimension to Emily's disappearance. The tree, a silent witness to centuries of history, seemed to hold a key to the unfolding mystery of Jeremiah Cooper.

In the following days, Jack delved into researching the oak tree's history. He poured over old land records, historical texts, and local folklore. The tree was indeed ancient, predating even the Pendle Witch Trials. Local legend held that it was a gathering spot for the accused witches, a place of clandestine meetings under the cover of night.

The more Jack learned, the more he became convinced that the oak tree was a conduit for paranormal occurrences. The sightings of a shadowy figure, believed to be Jeremiah Cooper, were most frequent near the tree. Jack theorized that the recent construction in Hillview Gardens might have disturbed some long-dormant energy linked to the tree and the tragic history it witnessed.

Seeking further insight, Jack arranged a private meeting with Sienna, the medium who had previously warned them about Jeremiah's powerful and tormented spirit. In her small, cluttered parlour, filled with the scent of incense and old books, Sienna listened intently to Jack's concerns.

After a moment of contemplative silence, she spoke in her soft, measured tone. "The oak tree is more than just a symbol; it's a spiritual anchor," she explained. "It's possible that the spirit of Jeremiah Cooper, bound by his unresolved guilt and duty, is drawn to the energy of the tree. The recent disturbances might have amplified this connection."

Jack broached his darkest fear - that Emily's disappearance was not just a case of a lost child but a paranormal abduction. Sienna's eyes narrowed thoughtfully. "If Jeremiah's spirit has grown strong enough, he may be attempting to recreate the past, taking what he perceives as a witch's descendant," she said gravely.

Determined to find answers, Jack called a meeting with the RIP Squad. They gathered in his living room, a stark contrast to their usual command centre setup. Jack laid out his findings and suspicions. The team listened, their expressions a mix of scepticism and concern. The idea of a paranormal abduction was daunting, yet the events at Hillview Gardens defied conventional explanations.

The team agreed that their first step was to conduct a thorough investigation around the oak tree, using all their available equipment. They planned to set up surveillance cameras, EMF meters, and thermal imaging tools to detect any unusual activity.

Jack knew they needed to involve the community. He organized a town hall meeting, intending to share their findings and enlist the residents' help. The meeting was tense, with emotions running high. Jack presented his theory with care, trying not to incite panic. He emphasized the need for vigilance and unity in the face of the unknown.

The investigation around the oak tree was set for a night when the moon was full, providing natural illumination to the eerie landscape. The RIP Squad worked with quiet efficiency, setting up their equipment under the watchful eyes of several curious residents.

As the night deepened, a palpable tension settled over the team. Every rustle of leaves, every shadow cast by the moonlight, seemed amplified. The equipment beeped and whirred, yet nothing out of the ordinary presented itself.

It wasn't until the early hours of the morning that they experienced a breakthrough. The thermal camera picked up an unusual cold spot moving around the tree. The EMF meter spiked simultaneously, and a faint, childlike giggle echoed through the still air, sending chills down everyone's spine.

The team gathered around the thermal camera, examining the footage. The cold spot was amorphous, shifting shape as it seemed to float around the tree. The giggle, captured on their audio equipment, was eerie, disembodied, and yet distinctly childlike.

Jack felt a surge of both hope and dread. "This could be a sign from Emily," he murmured, his mind racing with possibilities. Could Jeremiah's spirit have taken Emily? Was she trying to communicate with them?

As dawn approached, the team, exhausted but fuelled by the night's findings, discussed their next steps. They needed to analyse the footage and audio recordings in detail. They also agreed on the need for another séance, hoping to directly contact Jeremiah's spirit and, possibly, the spirit of Emily.

Word of the night's events spread quickly through Hillview Gardens. The community, already on edge, was now gripped by a mix of fear and fascination. While some residents whispered about leaving the estate, others rallied, offering help and support to the Harrises and the RIP Squad.

Jack stood alone by the oak tree, the first light of dawn casting long shadows on the ground. The weight of responsibility lay heavy on his shoulders. He was determined to uncover the truth, to bring Emily back, and to confront the restless spirit of Jeremiah Cooper that haunted not just the physical estate but the very souls of its residents.

As the first light of dawn cast a pale glow over Hillview Gardens, Jack's resolve solidified. The day ahead would be crucial in their quest to unravel the mystery surrounding Emily's disappearance and Jeremiah Cooper's haunting presence.

Back at the command centre, the RIP Squad convened to analyse the footage and audio from the night's investigation. The thermal imaging showed the cold spot near the oak tree with an almost human-like form. The audio recording of the childlike giggle was played repeatedly, each time sending a shiver down their spines.

Seeking further insight, Jack arranged for experts in paranormal phenomena and audio analysis to review their findings. The experts were baffled by the recordings, unable to provide a logical explanation for the cold spot or the disembodied giggle.

Despite the fear that gripped Hillview Gardens, the community's spirit of unity was stronger than ever. Volunteers organized daily search parties, combing the surrounding areas for any sign of Emily. Local businesses provided food and drinks for the search teams, and a fund was set up to support the Harris family.

The decision to conduct another séance was met with a mix of apprehension and hope. Sienna was once again enlisted to lead the session. The team prepared the Harris family living room, the site of the first disturbing message, for the séance. Candles were placed in a circle, and protective symbols were drawn.

As night fell, the RIP Squad and a few selected residents, including the Harrises, gathered for the séance. The room was charged with a tense expectancy. Sienna, more sombre than ever, began to chant, her voice rising and falling in a hypnotic rhythm.

The medium's body stiffened, her eyes rolling back as she made contact with the spiritual realm. In a voice that was not her own, she spoke, "Bound by guilt, bound by duty... the child is mine to keep." The chilling declaration, believed to be from Jeremiah's spirit, sent a wave of horror through the room.

Sienna, struggling to maintain control, then shifted her focus, attempting to reach Emily's spirit. The temperature in the room dropped noticeably, and a faint whisper could be heard. "Mommy... it's cold," a small, scared voice said, barely audible over the sound of weeping from the gathered group.

The séance continued, with Sienna channelling the tormented spirit of Jeremiah. His words were a mix of confusion and sorrow, speaking of his unending quest and the child he believed he must protect from witchcraft. It became clear that Jeremiah's spirit had taken Emily, mistaking her for a descendant of the witches he had once hunted.

As the séance concluded, the room felt suddenly empty, as if a weight had been lifted. Sienna exhausted, warned that while they had made contact, convincing Jeremiah to release Emily would be a formidable challenge. His spirit was entrenched in centuries-old beliefs and guilt.

For Laura and Michael Harris, the séance was both heartbreaking and illuminating. The possibility that their daughter was trapped in a spiritual realm was terrifying, yet the sound of her voice provided a glimmer of hope. They clung to each other, their faces a portrait of grief-stricken determination.

In the aftermath, Jack outlined a plan. They would conduct a ritual under the oak tree, aiming to appease Jeremiah's spirit and convince him to release Emily. The ritual would combine elements of historical witch trial practices with modern spiritualism, creating a bridge between Jeremiah's time and the present.

The community, now fully aware of the paranormal nature of Emily's disappearance, rallied behind Jack's plan. Preparations for the ritual began, with residents contributing in any way they could – from gathering materials to offering moral support.

As preparations for the ritual went underway, a sense of urgency permeated Hillview Gardens. Emily's fate hung in the balance, her life intertwined with the unresolved guilt and delusions of a centuries-old spirit. The community, once a picture of suburban tranquillity, had become the stage for a battle against a haunting born from the pages of history.

As the preparations for the ritual under the oak tree were underway, Jack pondered over the intricate complexities of the situation. The idea struck him during one of his late-night research sessions. If Jeremiah Cooper's spirit was indeed anchored to the past, specifically to his interactions with the Pendle witches, then perhaps those very witches could be the key to resolving the current crisis.

Jack, with a new sense of purpose, visited Sienna to discuss his idea. The notion of contacting the spirits of the Pendle witches was unorthodox, even in the realm of the paranormal, but the desperate situation called for unconventional methods. Sienna, intrigued by the idea, agreed to attempt to contact the witches during the ritual, hoping they might assist in convincing Jeremiah to release Emily.

As word of the plan spread, it elicited mixed reactions from the residents of Hillview Gardens. Some were sceptical, finding the idea too far-fetched, while others found a sense of hope in the possibility of reaching out to the spirits wronged by Jeremiah. The Harrises, driven by a desperate hope to see their daughter again, supported the plan wholeheartedly.

To strengthen their appeal to the witches, the RIP Squad delved into researching the lives of the women accused during the Pendle Witch Trials. They gathered names, stories, and any personal details they could find, hoping to establish a connection during the séance. Each story was a poignant reminder of the tragic injustices of the past.

Among the most enigmatic figures of the Pendle Witch Trials, Alice Nutter was a wealthy widow, which was unusual for someone accused of witchcraft at the time. Her story is marked by her unexpected involvement in the trials, as she was known for her quiet, reserved life. Rumours suggested she became entangled in the witch trials due to a family feud that tragically spiralled out of control.

Known for her unfortunate family legacy, Elizabeth Device, was caught in the web of accusations primarily due to her mother's (Demdike's) reputation as a witch. Elizabeth's story highlights the tragic consequences of guilt by association and the dangers of hysteria, as her own children were coerced into testifying against her.

Anne Whittle, often referred to as Old Chattox, was accused of using witchcraft for malevolent purposes, including murder. Her tale is one of desperation and poverty, as it was alleged, she turned to dark practices as a means to survive in harsh times. Her rivalry with another accused witch, Demdike, added to her notoriety.

The granddaughter of Demdike, Alizon Device's story is particularly tragic. A young woman accused of cursing a peddler, leading to his paralysis, her case was the catalyst for the Pendle Witch Trials. Alizon represents the tragic fate of the young and vulnerable caught in the merciless machinery of witch hunts.

Brother to Alizon, James Device was also swept up in the trials. His story reflects the vulnerability of those with physical and mental ailments in times of superstition, as he was said to be easily manipulated and coerced into confessing to witchcraft.

Katherine Hewitt (Mould Heels) was accused of attending a witches' sabbath and was one of the last to be swept up in the hysteria. Her nickname, Mould-Heels, came from a deformity in her leg. Katherine's story underscores the danger faced by those who were physically different or outsiders in their communities.

18

SPIRITUAL WARFARE

In the hushed stillness that followed the wail from the oak tree and Emily's distant cries, an intense, almost electric air enveloped Hillview Gardens. The spectral figures of the Pendle witches, their ethereal forms more defined in the moonlight, seemed to be communicating silently with Jeremiah's tormented spirit.

Amidst this supernatural tableau, Laura and Michael Harris stepped forward, their faces etched with a blend of hope and despair. Laura, her voice trembling with emotion, called out into the night, "Emily, we are here, we love you!" Beside her, Michael, his voice cracking, added, "Please, come back to us!"

At that moment, a chilling transformation occurred around the oak tree. The air shimmered, and the faint outline of Jeremiah Cooper materialized, his form wavering like a candle flame in the wind. His expression was one of confusion and anguish, a stark reminder of his troubled past and the pain that bound him to the earthly realm.

The lead figure among the Pendle witches, believed to be Alice Nutter, stepped forward. Her voice, though a mere whisper, carried a commanding presence. "Jeremiah Cooper," she began, "we, who suffered unjustly as you have, understand your pain. But this child is innocent, as were we. You must let her go."

A visible struggle seemed to take place within Jeremiah. His spectral form flickered wildly as he absorbed the witches' words. The air grew tense, the outcome hanging precariously in the balance.

It was the voice of Anne Whittle, Old Chattox, that seemed to reach a turning point. "Your quest for redemption," she said, "lies not in perpetuating the cycle of harm but in breaking it. Release the child, and find peace.

Jeremiah's spirit, after a moment that felt like an eternity, nodded slowly, his form beginning to dissipate. A sigh, almost like a release of a long-held breath, echoed through the night air.

Suddenly, the cold spot near the oak tree began to glow faintly. From within the light, a small figure emerged – Emily Harris. She looked bewildered but unharmed, as if waking from a deep sleep. Her parents rushed to her, enveloping her in a tight embrace, their tears of relief mingling with joy.

The crowd erupted in a mixture of cheers and sobs. The tension that had gripped Hillview Gardens for days was finally broken. Neighbours hugged each other, their relief palpable in the night air.

As the Harris family reunited, the spirits of the Pendle witches and Jeremiah Cooper faded into the night, their forms becoming less and less substantial until they vanished completely. A sense of peace, long absent, settled over the old oak tree and the surrounding gardens.

In the days that followed, Hillview Gardens slowly returned to normal, though the events left an indelible mark on the community. The story of Emily's disappearance and the involvement of historical spirits became a legend in the town, a tale of sorrow, redemption, and a community's unbreakable spirit.

Jack and the RIP Squad gathered one last time under the oak tree, reflecting on their journey. They had not only uncovered the truth behind a haunting but had also played a pivotal role in resolving a centuries-old cycle of pain and retribution. The experience had changed them, forging bonds that would last a lifetime.

The old oak tree, now just an ordinary tree in the daylight. Children play around it, their laughter a testament to the enduring resilience of innocence.

19

LIFTING THE SHADOW

The joy of Emily Harris's return to her family was palpable throughout Hillview Gardens, but an undercurrent of unease remained. The RIP Squad, acutely aware that the resolution with Jeremiah Cooper's spirit was perhaps only temporary, reconvened to address the lingering problem. The community, having witnessed the strange events surrounding Emily's disappearance and return, was more open to the idea of a deeper, more permanent solution.

They found themselves once again in Jack's living room, the familiar setting now shadowed by the uncertainty of their situation.

The room, usually a hub of strategy and planning, felt different this evening. The maps and notes that lined the walls seemed to echo their concerns back at them. The dim light filtering through the curtains cast long, contemplative shadows, mirroring the team's mood. Each member carried a look of deep thought, aware that their work was far from over.

Jack, sensing the heavy atmosphere, initiated the meeting with a tone of serious resolve. "We've brought Emily back, and for that, we can be grateful. But we all know that our job isn't done. Jeremiah's spirit may have retreated, but there's no guarantee he won't return." His words hung in the air, resonating with a truth they all recognized.

Jack paused, allowing his statement to resonate with the team. He walked slowly to the table that held their accumulated research - maps dotted with annotations, photographs capturing spectral images, and pages of historical references. His fingers brushed over these artifacts, a tactile connection to their journey.

"Our success with Emily was a significant step, but it's clear that we're dealing with something much larger than we initially thought," Jack added, turning the pages of a thick, aged book that lay open on the table. The book, an old tome on supernatural occurrences, was a recent addition to their collection, its pages worn from use.

"As much as we want to celebrate our victory, we can't lose sight of the bigger picture." Jack's tone was firm, a call to action that refocused the team. "Jeremiah Cooper's spirit is still tied to this place, and as long as that bond remains, the threat lingers over Hillview Gardens."

He looked around at his team, each member hanging on his every word. "We have a duty, not just to ourselves or to Emily, but to this entire community. We need to ensure that no one else falls victim to this haunting."

Jack's speech concluded with a quiet intensity, a reaffirmation of their commitment to the cause. The team, galvanized by his words, nodded in agreement, ready to continue their quest. They understood that the path ahead was fraught with unknowns, but guided by Jack's leadership, they were prepared to face whatever lay in store.

The team took turns recounting the recent surge in paranormal activity, especially the events culminating in Emily's disappearance and the subsequent ritual under the oak tree. They acknowledged that while Jeremiah's spirit seemed to have departed, the energy around the oak tree remained charged, a lingering reminder that the spiritual unrest might not be fully resolved.

Linda, who had been meticulously analysing her notes, contributed her insights. "The historical patterns we've seen with Jeremiah suggest a cyclical nature to his appearances. We've interrupted the cycle, but there's a real risk it could start again." Her analysis brought a data-driven perspective to the discussion, highlighting the potential risk of recurrence.

Each member then offered their perspective. Mason suggested a proactive approach, emphasizing the need to research more permanent solutions. Sarah, reflecting on her photographic evidence, noted the persistent anomalies around the oak tree. Theo brought the conversation back to the community's safety, underlining their responsibility to protect Hillview Gardens from further paranormal disturbances.

The discussion naturally flowed into potential strategies for a more definitive resolution. They explored various methods, both historical and contemporary, for dealing with restless spirits. From traditional cleansing rituals to modern paranormal interventions, the team considered each option's feasibility and impact.

As the meeting drew to a close, there was a collective agreement on the importance of finding a definitive solution. "We can't let Jeremiah's spirit linger in this state of unrest. It's not just about the safety of Hillview Gardens; it's about helping a tormented soul find peace," Jack concluded, succinctly capturing the dual purpose of their mission.

In the hushed atmosphere that followed Jack's opening remarks, a renewed sense of purpose began to take shape among the members of the RIP Squad. The gravity of Jack's words lingered in the air, emphasizing the weight of their responsibility not just to Emily, but to the entire community of Hillview Gardens.

As the team delved into discussion, the room became a hive of activity. Maps were spread out on the table, each marked with areas of significant paranormal activity. Photographs of the oak tree, now a symbol of both hope and haunting, were passed around, each member studying them intently.

Mason, always analytical, was the first to break the contemplative silence. "We need to consider all our options. Whatever we did at the ritual worked, but it was a temporary solution. Jeremiah is still out there, and we don't know when or how he might manifest again."

Sarah, who had been quietly flicking through her collection of photographs, looked up. "The patterns we've seen so far, the cold spots, the apparitions, they're all cantered around that tree. It's like it's a beacon for paranormal energy."

Linda nodded in agreement. "The historical significance of the tree can't be underestimated. It's been a part of Hillview Gardens' landscape for centuries, witnessing the town's evolution. There's a lot of residual energy there."

Jack proposed reaching out to more experts in the field. "We need to consult with historians and paranormal researchers. There might be rituals or historical precedents we can use to our advantage," he suggested.

Theo, looking thoughtful, added, "We also need to involve the community. They've seen what's happening, and their support will be crucial. Plus, they have a right to be a part of this. It's their town, their history too."

The team spent hours brainstorming, considering various strategies that combined historical research, paranormal science, and community involvement. The plan that began to emerge was multi-faceted, aiming to address both the spiritual unrest and the community's need for closure.

Jack decided to hold a series of town hall meetings. "We need to educate the residents, prepare them for what's to come. This isn't just our fight; it's theirs too," he asserted. The meetings would serve to inform the community about their findings and involve them in the planning process.

One of the central elements of their plan was a large-scale cleansing ritual, one that would involve the entire community. The ritual would be both a symbolic and practical effort to cleanse Hillview Gardens of the lingering paranormal energy.

They gather materials, coordinate with local leaders, and set the stage for what they hope will be the final resolution of the haunting of Hillview Gardens.

They agreed to reconvene in a few days to pool their findings and formulate a comprehensive plan. The meeting ended with a renewed sense of determination. The members of the RIP Squad left Jack's house, stepping out under the starlit sky of Hillview Gardens. In the distance, the silhouette of the oak tree stood as a silent reminder of the task that lay ahead – a symbol of both the challenges they had faced and the ones still to come.

20

THE SHADOW STRIKES BACK

As the preparations for the community-wide ritual at Hillview Gardens progressed, an air of cautious optimism pervaded the estate. The RIP Squad, at the forefront of these efforts, worked tirelessly, coordinating with community leaders and ensuring every detail was accounted for. However, unbeknownst to them, a dark undercurrent was stirring, a backlash from the restless spirit they sought to appease.

It began subtly, initially dismissed as fatigue due to their relentless work. Linda was the first to feel unwell, a sudden onset of dizziness and nausea that forced her to leave one of the planning meetings early. By the next morning, Mason reported a severe headache that blurred his vision, Theo complained of feeling queasy and Sarah found herself battling waves of unexplained weakness.

Jack, observing his team's deteriorating condition, felt a growing sense of alarm. The symptoms were too sudden, too synchronized to be a coincidence. He suspected they were dealing with something beyond the realm of the ordinary – a targeted strike from Jeremiah's spirit.

Worried about the team's wellbeing, Jack arranged an emergency meeting with Sierra. In her candle-lit parlour, the air heavy with the scent of burning sage, he explained the situation. Sierra, her expression grave, listened intently.

After a moment of contemplation, she spoke. "It's not uncommon for spirits with unfinished business to lash out, especially when they feel threatened," she said. "Jeremiah's spirit is potent, fuelled by centuries of guilt and anger. He might be perceiving your efforts as a direct challenge to his presence."

Despite the risk, the team decided to press on with their plans. They understood the stakes were high, not just for themselves but for the entire community of Hillview Gardens. "We can't let fear dictate our actions," Jack stated firmly, a sentiment echoed by the rest of the team, even in their weakened state.

Over the following days, the team's condition worsened. Linda was confined to her bed, wracked with severe migraines. Mason's vision problems escalated, accompanied by disorienting bouts of vertigo. Sarah, struggling with extreme fatigue, found herself unable to concentrate or stay awake for long periods. Theo's condition seemed to be getting worse by the hour, unable to hold anything down.

Concerned for their health, Jack insisted they seek medical attention. However, the doctors were baffled. Tests and scans revealed no physical cause for their symptoms, leaving them with more questions than answers.

Word of the team's illness spread through Hillview Gardens, casting a shadow over the ritual preparations. The community, already on edge due to the paranormal occurrences, began to fear for their safety. Rumours swirled, some speculating that the illness was a warning from Jeremiah's spirit, others wondering if they were next.

Despite their ailments, the team continued to work on the ritual plans, albeit at a slower pace. Jack found himself doubling his efforts, coordinating with community leaders and reassuring residents, all while keeping a watchful eye on his team.

In an attempt to counteract the negative energy, Sierra conducted a protection ritual for the team. She used a combination of herbs, crystals, and incantations, aiming to shield them from further spiritual harm. While the ritual provided some relief, it was clear that the only real solution was to confront Jeremiah's spirit directly.

On the eve of the planned community ritual, the team gathered at Jack's house. They were a picture of determination, albeit physically weakened. Jack looked at his team, their faces drawn but resolute, and felt a surge of pride. "Tomorrow, we end this," he said, his voice steady. "For ourselves, for Emily, for Hillview Gardens."

The team in a moment of quiet reflection, were each lost in their thoughts about the upcoming confrontation. The night air was still, the only sound the gentle rustling of leaves from the oak tree in the distance.

The night was still as the RIP Squad sat in Jack's living room, each member grappling with their own thoughts and fears. The silence was a stark contrast to the usual buzz of strategy and discussion that had filled this space. Now, it was as if the shadow of Jeremiah's malevolent presence loomed over them, a tangible reminder of the battle they were about to face.

Dawn broke with a sky painted in hues of orange and pink, casting a new light over Hillview Gardens. It was the day of the ritual, and despite their weakened state, the team prepared to confront Jeremiah's spirit. They gathered their equipment and made their way to the oak tree, the site of so many strange occurrences and now the stage for their final stand.

As they arrived, they were met by the sight of the community coming together. Residents had gathered around the oak tree, some setting up chairs, others laying out food and drinks. Despite the underlying fear, there was a sense of solidarity that filled the air. The community was ready to stand with the RIP Squad, to reclaim their home from the clutches of the past.

Sienna, once again at the forefront, began the ritual. Her voice, strong and clear, cut through the morning air. She called upon the spirits of peace and protection, her words weaving a tapestry of ancient incantations and modern affirmations.

Each member of the team had a specific role in the ritual. Linda, despite her migraine, was in charge of monitoring the EMF readings, her equipment set up around the perimeter of the oak tree. Mason, with his blurred vision, relied on his other senses, listening intently to the sounds of the ritual and the reactions of the crowd. Sarah, fighting off waves of exhaustion, manned the camera, documenting every moment. Theo was just Theo, he was quiet but managed to force himself to monitor a thermal imaging camera.

Jack was the anchor, his presence a steady force amidst the swirling energy of the ritual. He moved through the crowd, offering words of encouragement, his gaze frequently returning to the oak tree, as if trying to pierce the veil between worlds.

As the ritual reached its climax, a hush fell over the crowd. The air around the oak tree shimmered, and a chill wind swept through the gathering. It was as if the very fabric of reality was thinning, opening a gateway to the other side.

Sienna's voice rose in a final, commanding chant. The atmosphere was charged with anticipation and fear. Then, there was a shift, a feeling of release, as if a pressure had been lifted. From the corner of his eye, Jack saw a shadowy figure near the tree – Jeremiah, his form less menacing, more ethereal.

Sienna spoke directly to the spirit, her words a mixture of forgiveness and release. "Jeremiah Cooper, your duty is fulfilled. Find peace in the light." Slowly, the figure began to fade, the air around it growing lighter, less oppressive.

As the figure of Jeremiah dissipated, a collective sigh rose from the crowd. The sense of relief was palpable. People hugged, some cried, and others simply stood in silent reflection. The ritual, it seemed, had worked.

In the days following the ritual, the team's health began to improve. The mysterious symptoms that had plagued them gradually receded. Linda's migraines subsided, Mason's vision cleared, and Sarah's energy returned. Theo said he could eat a scabby horse. It was as if Jeremiah's departing spirit had lifted the curse he had unwittingly cast upon them.

21

A NEW BEGINNING

As the dust settled on the events that had shaken Hillview Gardens, life slowly began to return to normal. The once-ominous oak tree now stood as a benign landmark, its shadow no longer casting fear among the residents. Children's laughter once again filled the air, and neighbours resumed their daily routines, the sense of community stronger than ever. For the RIP Squad, however, the resolution of the haunting marked not an end, but a new beginning.

People are out tending to their gardens, kids are riding bikes, and there's a general sense of peace. The recent events have become the talk of the town, with residents sharing their experiences and stories in local cafes and shops.

As the sun dipped below the horizon, casting a golden hue over the quaint town of Hillview Gardens, Sienna, the local medium who had played a crucial role in resolving the haunting, felt a lingering sense of unfinished business. In the quiet of her candle-lit parlour, she contemplated the spirits of the Pendle witches, who had been instrumental in helping release Emily and pacify Jeremiah Cooper's troubled soul. It dawned upon her that these spirits, too, deserved peace.

Sienna began to plan a ritual, one that would not only help the witches find peace but also allow the community to acknowledge and celebrate their part in the town's history. She envisioned it as a ceremony of closure and remembrance, a way to honour the spirits that had been wronged centuries ago.

On the eve of the ritual, Sienna prepared her parlour. She arranged a circle of candles, each representing one of the Pendle witches. The room was filled with the scent of sage and lavender, herbs known for their cleansing and calming properties. In the centre of the circle, she placed an old, leather-bound book containing records of the witch trials, a symbol of the history they were acknowledging.

As the clock struck four in the morning, marking the time when the veil between worlds was thinnest, Sienna began the ritual. She started by calling out the names of the witches, her voice a soft, melodic chant that filled the room. "Alice Nutter, Elizabeth Device, Anne Whittle, Alizon Device, James Device, Katherine Hewitt," she called, her voice imbued with respect and empathy.

She then spoke a heartfelt invocation, "Spirits of the past, wronged and misunderstood, hear my call. Tonight, we seek to offer you peace and release. Your pain is recognized, and your stories are not forgotten."

Sierra then lit the candles, one for each of the witches. The flames flickered, casting dancing shadows on the walls, as if responding to her words. She continued, "May these flames symbolize the light of truth and understanding, illuminating your path to the peace you so rightly deserve."

She spent the next few hours in quiet meditation, her thoughts focused on sending positive, peaceful energy to the spirits. As the candles burned down, the atmosphere in the room shifted, feeling lighter, as if a weight had been lifted.

In the following days, Sierra shared her experience with the community of Hillview Gardens. Moved by her gesture and the role the witches had played in their recent ordeal, the town decided to hold an annual celebration in their honour.

The celebration became a cherished tradition in Hillview Gardens, a day of remembrance and gratitude. It featured historical reenactments, storytelling sessions, and a candlelight vigil similar to Sierra's ritual. Local historians provided context, sharing the true stories of the Pendle witches, dispelling myths, and fostering understanding.

Each year, as the celebration approached, the town was adorned with decorations reflecting the era of the witch trials. The centrepiece was a display around the old oak tree, now a symbol of reconciliation and peace. Residents gathered to pay homage, laying flowers at the base of the tree and lighting candles in memory of the witches.

The annual celebration not only served as a reminder of the town's rich and complex history but also as a testament to its ability to heal and grow from its past. It became a day of unity and reflection, a time for the community to come together and acknowledge the darker chapters of history while celebrating the light of understanding and forgiveness.

Through this story, Sierra's ritual and the subsequent annual celebration became a powerful symbol of reconciliation and peace, transforming the legacy of fear and misunderstanding into one of respect and remembrance.

At Jack's house, the RIP Squad gathered for what had become their regular meeting. The mood was light, a stark contrast to their previous gatherings. They shared stories and laughed, but there was an underlying sense of purpose in their conversation.

The events at Hillview Gardens had garnered significant media attention, casting a spotlight on the RIP Squad. Their successful resolution of the haunting had made them somewhat local celebrities. Articles about their bravery and expertise in handling the paranormal situation were featured in newspapers and on local television.

This newfound recognition brought with it a realization. The team acknowledged that their unique blend of skills could be used to help others facing similar paranormal situations. "We've got something special here," Jack said. "We've helped our community, but there are others out there who are facing their own nightmares. We can help them."

The team discussed the possibility of formally offering their services to others dealing with paranormal phenomena. They decided to create a network, utilizing their contacts and the publicity they had gained to reach out to those in need.

They began to lay the groundwork for what would become an official paranormal investigation team. Linda took charge of the research and documentation, Mason handled the logistics and coordination, Sarah managed communications and media relations, and Theo focused on the technical and equipment aspects. Jack, as always, was the leader, the glue holding the team together.

The Hillview Gardens community, grateful for the team's efforts, offered their support. Local businesses provided funding and resources, and residents volunteered their skills and time. The spirit of community that had been so crucial in resolving the haunting continued to thrive.

The RIP Squad were gathered around a map, now dotted with locations outside of Hillview Gardens. They were no longer just a group of friends united by a local haunting; they had become a team with a purpose, ready to face whatever mysteries lay ahead.

As the evening light faded, casting a soft glow over Jack's living room, the team shared a quiet moment of contemplation. They had embarked on a journey that would take them into the unknown, but they were ready. They had each other, and they had a newfound calling – to help those haunted by the shadows of the paranormal.

Don't miss out!

Visit the website below and you can sign up to receive emails whenever Blake Patrick publishes a new book. There's no charge and no obligation.

https://books2read.com/r/B-A-DEZBB-GFWRC

BOOKS 2 READ

Connecting independent readers to independent writers.

Also by Blake Patrick

Chronicles of the Eternal Nile
Whispers of the Nile

The RIP Squad Chronicles
Pendle's Curse

Standalone
Fractured Shields
Hidden Cargo
Shadow of a Witch
Shadows and Solace
Whispered Promises

Watch for more at blake-patrick.co.uk.